YOUNG PUFFIN MODERN CLASSICS

Mr Majeika and *Mr Majeika and the Music Teacher*

Humphrey Carpenter is the author of the Mr Majeika stories for children. He was born and educated in Oxford and worked for the BBC before becoming a full-time writer in 1975. He has published award-winning biographies of J. R. R. Tolkien, C. S. Lewis, W. H. Auden, Benjamin Britten and others, and is the co-author, with his wife, Mari Prichard, of *The Oxford Companion to Children's Literature*. From 1994 to 1996 he directed the Cheltenham Festival of Literature. He has written plays for radio and the theatre, including a dramatization of *Gulliver's Travels* (1995), and for many years ran a young people's drama group, the Mushy Pea Theatre Company. He has two daughters.

Once you have finished reading *Mr Majeika* and *Mr Majeika and the Music Teacher* you may be interested in reading the Afterword by Wendy Cooling on page 177.

Other books by Humphrey Carpenter

MR MAJEIKA AND THE DINNER LADY
MR MAJEIKA AND THE GHOST TRAIN
MR MAJEIKA AND THE HAUNTED HOTEL
MR MAJEIKA AND THE SCHOOL BOOK WEEK
MR MAJEIKA AND THE SCHOOL CARETAKER
MR MAJEIKA AND THE SCHOOL INSPECTOR
MR MAJEIKA AND THE SCHOOL PLAY
MR MAJEIKA AND THE SCHOOL TRIP
MR MAJEIKA VANISHES
MR MAJEIKA'S POSTBAG

THE PUFFIN BOOK OF CLASSIC
CHILDREN'S STORIES (ED.)

HUMPHREY CARPENTER

Mr Majeika

AND

Mr Majeika and the Music Teacher

ILLUSTRATED BY FRANK RODGERS

PUFFIN BOOKS

PUFFIN BOOKS

Published by the Penguin Group
Penguin Books Ltd, 27 Wrights Lane, London W8 5TZ, England
Penguin Putnam Inc., 375 Hudson Street, New York, New York 10014, USA
Penguin Books Australia Ltd, Ringwood, Victoria, Australia
Penguin Books Canada Ltd, 10 Alcorn Avenue, Toronto, Ontario, Canada M4V 3B2
Penguin Books (NZ) Ltd, Private Bag 102902, NSMC, Auckland, New Zealand

Penguin Books Ltd, Registered Offices: Harmondsworth, Middlesex, England

Mr Majeika first published by Kestrel Books 1984
Published in Puffin Books 1985
Mr Majeika and the Music Teacher first published by Viking Kestrel 1986
Published in Puffin Books 1987
This edition published 1999
3

Set in 17/22pt Monotype Bembo
Typeset by Rowland Phototypesetting Ltd,
Bury St Edmunds, Suffolk
Printed in England by Clays Ltd, St Ives plc

British Library Cataloguing in Publication Data
A CIP catalogue record for this book is available from the British Library

ISBN 0-141-30281-X

Mr Majeika

CHAPTER I

The Carpet-Bicycle

It was Monday morning, it was pouring with rain, and it was everyone's first day back at St Barty's Primary School after the Christmas holidays. That's why Class Three were in a bad temper.

Pandora Green had been rude to

Melanie, so Melanie was crying (though Melanie always found *something* to cry about). Hamish Bigmore was trying to pick a quarrel with Thomas and Pete, the twins. And Mr Potter, the head teacher, was very cross because the new teacher for Class Three hadn't turned up.

'I can't think where he is,' he grumbled at Class Three. 'He should have been here at nine o'clock for the beginning of school. And now it's nearly ten, and I should be teaching Class Two. We'll have to open the folding doors and let you share the lesson with them.'

Class Three groaned. They thought themselves very important people, and didn't in the least want to share a lesson with Class Two, who were just babies.

'Bother this thing,' muttered Mr

Potter, struggling with the folding doors that separated the classrooms.

'*I'll* help you, Mr Potter,' said Hamish Bigmore, who didn't really want to help at all, but just to be a nuisance as usual. And then everyone else began to shout: 'Don't let Hamish Bigmore do it, he's no good, let *me* help,' so that in a moment there was uproar.

But suddenly silence fell. And there was a gasp.

Mr Potter was still fiddling with the folding doors, so he didn't see what was happening. But Class Three did.

One of the big windows in the classroom slid open all by itself, and *something* flew in.

It was a man on a magic carpet.

There could be no doubt about that. Class Three knew a magic carpet when they saw one. After all, they'd read *Aladdin* and all that sort of stuff. There are magic carpets all over the place in *Aladdin*. But this wasn't *Aladdin*. This was St Barty's Primary School on a wet Monday morning. And magic carpets don't turn up in schools. Class Three knew that. So they stared.

The carpet hung in the air for a moment, as if it wasn't sure what to do. Then it came down on the floor with a bump. 'Ow!' said the man sitting on it.

He was quite old, and he had a pointed beard and very bright eyes, behind a pair of glasses. His hair and clothes were wet from the rain. On the whole he looked quite ordinary – except for the fact that he was sitting on a magic carpet.

'I just can't manage it,' said Mr Potter,

still pushing at the folding doors. 'I'll have to go and get the caretaker.'

Then he saw the man on the carpet.

'What – how – eh?' said Mr Potter. Words usually deserted Mr Potter at difficult moments.

The man on the carpet scrambled to his feet. 'Majeika,' he said politely, offering his hand.

Mr Potter took the hand. 'Majeika?' he repeated, puzzled. Then a look of understanding dawned on his face. 'Ah,' he said, 'Mr Majeika!' He turned to Class Three. 'Boys and girls,' he said, 'I want you to meet Mr Majeika. He's your new teacher.'

For a moment there was silence. Then Melanie began to cry: 'Boo-hoo! I'm *frightened* of him! He came on a magic carpet!'

'What's the matter, Melanie?' snapped Mr Potter. 'I can't hear a word you're saying. It sounded like "magic carpet" or some such nonsense.' He turned briskly to Mr Majeika. 'Now, you're rather late, Mr Majeika. You might have telephoned me.'

'I'm so sorry,' said Mr Majeika. 'You see, my magic carpet took a wrong turning. It's normally quite good at finding the way, but I think the rain must have got into it. I do beg your pardon.'

'Never mind,' said Mr Potter. 'And now . . . Wait a minute, did I hear you say *magic carpet*?'

It was Mr Majeika's turn to look bothered. 'Oh, did I really say that? How very silly of me. A complete slip of the tongue. I meant – *bicycle*, of course. I came on a bicycle.'

'Quite so,' said Mr Potter. 'Bicycle, of course . . .' His voice tailed off. He was staring at the magic carpet. 'What's that?' he said rather faintly.

'That?' said Mr Majeika cheerily. 'That's my magic –' He cleared his throat. 'Oh dear, my mistake again. *That's my bicycle.*' And as he said these last words, he pointed a finger at the magic carpet.

There was a funny sort of humming noise, and the carpet rolled itself up and turned into a bicycle.

Mr Majeika leant cheerily against the handlebars and rang the bicycle bell. 'Nice bike, isn't it?' he said, smiling at Mr Potter.

You could have heard a pin drop.

Mr Potter turned rather white. 'I – I don't think I feel very well,' he said at last.

'I – I don't seem to be able to tell the difference between a carpet and a bicycle.'

Mr Majeika smiled even more cheerily. 'Never mind, a very easy mistake to make. And now I think it's time I began to teach our young friends here.'

Mr Potter wiped his forehead with his handkerchief. 'What? Oh – yes – of course,' he muttered faintly, backing to the door. 'Yes, yes, please do begin. Can't tell a bicycle from a carpet . . .' he mumbled to himself as he left the room.

'Now then,' said Mr Majeika to Class Three, 'to work!'

CHAPTER 2

Chips for Everyone

Never had Class Three been so quiet as they were for the rest of that lesson. They sat in absolute silence as Mr Majeika told them what work he planned to give them for the rest of that term.

Not that any of them was really

listening to what he was saying. It actually sounded very ordinary, with stuff about nature-study, and the kings and queens of England, and special projects, and that sort of thing, just like all the other teachers. But they couldn't take it in. Each of them was thinking about just one thing: the magic carpet.

When break came, and they were all having milk and biscuits, they whispered about it.

'I *saw* it,' whispered Pandora Green's best friend, Jody.

'So did I,' said Thomas and Pete together. 'It *was* a magic carpet.'

'If you ask *me*,' said Hamish Bigmore, 'it was a mass hallucination.' Hamish Bigmore was always learning long words just so that he could show them off.

'What's that mean?' said Thomas and Pete suspiciously.

'It's when you think you've seen something and you haven't,' said Hamish Bigmore. 'People get them when they're walking across the desert. They think they see a pool of water, and when they get there, there's only sand.'

'But we're not in the desert, you idiot,' said Thomas. 'And we didn't see water, we saw a magic carpet, and it turned into a bicycle. And we *all* saw it, so how could we have imagined it?'

'That's why it's called *mass* hallucination,' said Hamish Bigmore grandly. '*Mass* means lots of people. So idiot yourself!'

And they might have believed him, if it wasn't for what happened at dinner.

Most of Class Three ate school dinner, but some of them were sent to school with packed lunches which their mothers had made at home, and which they ate at a separate table. Thomas and Pete did this, and so did Jody.

So did Wim. He was Thomas and Pete's younger brother. He was in the nursery class, so Thomas and Pete only saw him at dinner time. He was really called William, but 'Wim' was how he said his own name, so that was what everyone called him.

Wim was tucking happily into a piece of egg and bacon flan, which was his favourite lunch. Thomas and Pete were talking to Jody while they ate theirs. 'What do you think about the magic carpet?' they asked her for the hundredth time.

'Ssh, here he comes!' whispered Jody.

Mr Majeika was approaching their table. He sat down next to them. 'Hello,' he said in a friendly manner. 'Was there anything you wanted to ask me about the lessons for this term?'

Thomas, Pete and Jody looked at each other. Of course there was something they wanted to ask him!

Suddenly there was a wail from Wim. He had dropped his egg and bacon flan on the floor.

Thomas and Pete looked gloomily at each other. They would have to give Wim some of their own dinner.

'My poor chap, most unfortunate,' said Mr Majeika. He bent down and picked up the mess of egg and bacon flan. 'We must see what we can do with this,' he said to Wim. 'Tell me, my young friend, what is your favourite food?'

Wim thought for a moment. Then he said: 'Chips.'

'Ah,' said Mr Majeika, shutting his eyes for a moment, and pointing at Wim's plate. 'Chips.'

'Oo!' said Wim suddenly. And no wonder, for on his plate, where the broken bits of flan had been, stood a huge pile of steaming hot chips.

'Oh!' said Thomas, Pete and Jody.

'Would you like some too, my young friends?' said Mr Majeika. Thomas, Pete and Jody nodded, and suddenly, out of nowhere, there were piles of chips on their plates too.

'Gosh!' said Thomas, Pete and Jody.

Suddenly another voice broke in. 'What's this? You know we don't allow chips here at dinner time.' It was Mr Potter.

He had come up behind Mr Majeika without anyone noticing. 'It's a very strict rule,' he said. 'Parents may send their children to school with sandwiches or other cold food, but I will not allow boys and girls to go out and buy chips during the dinner hour.'

'But we didn't buy them,' began Thomas.

'No, no,' interrupted Mr Majeika quickly. 'They certainly didn't buy them. It was *I* who provided them, not knowing the school rules. It won't happen again.'

'Well,' said Mr Potter crossly, 'please don't let it.' He walked off.

Mr Majeika sighed. 'Oh dear,' he said, 'I think I've got a lot to learn in my new job. You see, I'm not at all experienced at being a teacher. I've always worked as, well . . . something else.'

Thomas hesitated for a moment, then plucked up courage to say: 'Do you mean you were a *wizard*?'

Mr Majeika nodded. 'I might as well admit it,' he said. 'I worked as one for years, but then I began to get a bit rusty on my spells, and recently there hasn't been much business. People don't believe much in wizards nowadays, so naturally they don't often pay them to do some work. So in the end I just had to get another kind of job. That's why I'm here. And now I really *must* remember that I'm a teacher, and not a wizard at all. And you must all help me. You mustn't try to persuade me to do any –' He hesitated.

'Any magic?' said Pete.

Mr Majeika nodded. 'You must let me be an *ordinary teacher*,' he said. 'Do you promise?'

They all nodded. But each of them thought it would be a very difficult promise to keep.

★

By three-fifteen that day, when afternoon school was nearly at an end, nothing else out of the ordinary had happened in Class Three. In fact the afternoon would have ended very boringly if it hadn't been for Hamish Bigmore.

Hamish had been put to sit next to Melanie, which was a bad thing for Melanie, as Hamish liked nothing better than to make her cry.

Sure enough, when there were only

a few more minutes to go, Melanie started to sob. 'Boo-hoo! Hamish Bigmore is jabbing me with his ruler!'

Hamish Bigmore said he wasn't, but Mr Majeika moved fast enough to get to the scene of the crime before Hamish had time to hide the ruler. 'Put it down!' said Mr Majeika.

'Shan't,' said Hamish Bigmore.

There was silence, and everyone in Class Three remembered how Hamish Bigmore had refused to do as he was told by last term's teacher. It was mostly because of him that she had left the school.

'Put it down,' said Mr Majeika again.

'Shan't,' said Hamish Bigmore for a second time.

'Then,' said Mr Majeika slowly, '*I*

shall make you wish very much that you had put it down.'

And Hamish Bigmore screamed.

'A snake! Help! Help!' he shouted. And there fell from his hand something that certainly wasn't a ruler.

It was a long grey-green snake with patterned markings and a forked tongue. Its mouth was open and it was hissing.

In a moment everyone else was shouting too, and clambering on to the desks, and doing anything they could to get out of its reach. But not Mr Majeika.

He stepped calmly up to the snake, knelt down, and picked it up. And as his hand touched it, it turned back into a ruler.

'What are you frightened of?' he

asked Hamish Bigmore. 'This is only your ruler. But perhaps next time you will do as you are told.'

He gave the ruler back to Hamish Bigmore, who dropped it fearfully on his desk and shrank away from it.

A moment later the bell rang, and school was over for the day. Class Three usually rushed outside as soon as they heard the bell. But today they were quiet as mice.

'He *said* he didn't want to do any magic,' said Thomas to Pete on the way home.

'I think he just forgets about that now and then,' said Pete. 'After all, if you've been a wizard for years, it can't be easy stopping overnight.'

'Mr Majeika . . .' said Thomas thoughtfully to himself. 'Do you know,

I don't think that's his real name.'

'No,' said Pete. 'I think he ought to be called Mr Magic.'

CHAPTER 3

Hamish Goes Swimming

In fact for a long time after that Mr Magic, as all Class Three were soon calling him, *didn't* forget that he was meant to be a teacher, and not a wizard. Nothing peculiar happened for weeks and weeks, and the lessons went on just as they would have with any other teacher. The magic carpet, the chips, and the snake seemed like a dream.

Then Hamish Bigmore came to stay at Thomas and Pete's house.

This wasn't at all a good thing, at least not for Thomas and Pete. But they had no choice. Hamish Bigmore's mother and father had to go away for a few days, and Thomas and Pete's mum had offered to look after Hamish until they came back. She never asked Thomas and Pete what they thought about the idea until it was too late.

Hamish Bigmore behaved even worse than they had expected. He found all their favourite books and games, which they had tried to hide from him, and spoilt them or left them lying about the house where they got trodden on and broken. He pulled the stuffing out of

Wim's favourite teddy bear, bounced up and down so hard on the garden climbing-frame that it bent, and talked for hours and hours after the light had been put out at night, so that Thomas and Pete couldn't get to sleep. 'It's awful,' said Thomas. 'I wish that something really nasty would happen to him.'

And it did.

Hamish Bigmore was behaving just as badly at school as at Thomas and Pete's house. The business of the ruler turning into a snake had frightened him for a few days, but no longer than that, and now he was up to his old tricks again, doing anything rather than listen to Mr Majeika and behave properly.

On the Wednesday morning before Hamish Bigmore's mother and father were due to come home, Mr Majeika was giving Class Three a nature-study lesson, with the tadpoles in the glass tank that sat by his desk. Hamish Bigmore was being ruder than ever.

'Does anyone know how long tadpoles take to turn into frogs?' Mr Majeika asked Class Three.

'Haven't the slightest idea,' said Hamish Bigmore.

'Please,' said Melanie, holding up her hand, 'I don't think it's very long. Only a few weeks.'

'*You* should know,' sneered Hamish Bigmore. 'You look just like a tadpole yourself.'

Melanie began to cry.

'Be quiet, Hamish Bigmore,' said Mr Majeika. 'Melanie is quite right. It all happens very quickly. The tadpoles grow arms and legs, and very soon –'

'I shouldn't think they'll grow at all if they see *you* staring in at them through the glass,' said Hamish Bigmore to Mr Majeika. 'Your face would frighten them to death!'

'Hamish Bigmore, I have had enough of you,' said Mr Majeika. 'Will you stop behaving like this?'

'No, I won't!' said Hamish Bigmore.

Mr Majeika pointed a finger at him.

And Hamish Bigmore vanished.

There was complete silence. Class Three stared at the empty space where Hamish Bigmore had been sitting.

Then Pandora Green pointed at the glass tank, and began to shout: 'Look! Look! A frog! A frog! One of the tadpoles has turned into a frog!'

Mr Majeika looked closely at the tank.

Then he put his head in his hands. He seemed very upset.

'No, Pandora,' he said. 'It isn't one of the tadpoles. It's Hamish Bigmore.'

For a moment, Class Three were struck dumb. Then everyone burst out laughing. 'Hooray! Hooray! Hamish Bigmore has been turned into a frog! Good old Mr Magic!'

'It looks like Hamish Bigmore, doesn't it?' Pete said to Thomas. Certainly the frog's expression looked very much like Hamish's face. And it was splashing noisily around the tank and carrying on in the silly sort of way that Hamish did.

Mr Majeika looked very worried. 'Oh dear, oh dear,' he kept saying.

'Didn't you mean to do it?' asked Jody.

Mr Majeika shook his head. 'Certainly not. I quite forgot myself. It was a complete mistake.'

'Well,' said Thomas, 'you can turn him back again, can't you?'

Mr Majeika shook his head again. 'I'm not at all sure that I can,' he said.

Thomas and Pete looked at him in astonishment.

'You see,' he went on, 'it was an old spell, something I learnt years and years ago and thought I'd forgotten. I don't know what were the exact words I used. And, as I am sure you understand, it's not possible to undo a spell unless you know exactly what the words were.'

'So Hamish Bigmore may have to stay a frog?' said Pete. 'That's the best thing I've heard for ages!'

Mr Majeika shook his head. 'For you,

maybe, but not for him. I'll have to try and do *something*.' And he began to mutter a whole series of strange-sounding words under his breath.

All kinds of things began to happen. The room went dark, and the floor seemed to rock. Green smoke came out of an empty jar on Mr Majeika's desk. He tried some more words, and this time there was a small thunderstorm in the sky outside. But nothing happened to the frog.

'Oh, dear,' sighed Mr Majeika, 'what *am* I going to do?'

CHAPTER 4

The Frog's Princess

Thomas and Pete thought for a moment. Then Thomas said: 'Don't worry about it yet, Mr Magic. Hamish Bigmore's parents are away, and he's staying with us. You've got two days to find the right spell before they come back and expect to find him.'

'Two days,' repeated Mr Majeika. 'In that case there is a chance. We shall simply have to see what happens at midnight.'

'Midnight?' asked Jody.

'My friend,' said Mr Majeika, 'surely you know that in fairy stories everything returns to its proper shape when the clock strikes twelve?'

'Cinderella's coach,' said Jody.

'Exactly,' answered Mr Majeika. 'But one can't be certain of it. There's only a chance. I'll stay here tonight, and see what happens.'

And with that, Class Three went home.

Thomas and Pete felt that really they should have taken Hamish Bigmore home with them, even if he *was* a frog. After all, he was supposed to be staying with them.

'But,' said Pete, 'it's not easy carrying frogs. He might escape, and jump into a river or something, and we'd never see him again.'

'And a very good thing too,' said Thomas.

'You can't say that,' remarked Pete. 'He may be only Hamish Bigmore to you and me, but to his mum and dad he's darling little Hamie, or something like that. And just think what it would be like to be mother and father to a frog. Going to the shops, and the library, and that sort of thing, and people saying: "Oh, Mrs Bigmore, what a *sweet* little frog you're carrying in that jar." And Hamish's mum having to say: "Oh, Mrs Smith, that's not just a frog, that's our son Hamish."'

When Thomas and Pete's mum saw

them at the school gates the first thing she said was 'Where's Hamish?', and they had quite a time persuading her that Hamish wouldn't be coming home with them that afternoon, or staying the night, but was visiting friends, and was being perfectly well taken care of.

'Who are these friends?' she asked suspiciously. 'What's their name?'

'Tadpoles,' said Pete, without thinking.

'Idiot,' whispered Thomas, kicking him. 'We don't know their name,' he told his mum. 'But Mr Majeika, our new teacher, arranged it, so it must be all right.'

'Oh, did he?' said their mum. 'Well, he might have told me. But I suppose I shouldn't fuss.' And she took them home.

When they got back to school the next morning, Hamish Bigmore was still a frog.

'Nothing happened at all,' said Mr Majeika gloomily.

He tried to make Class Three get on with their ordinary work, but it wasn't much use. Nobody had their minds on anything but Hamish Bigmore, swimming up and down in his tank.

Everyone kept making suggestions to Mr Majeika.

'Mr Magic, couldn't you just get a magic wand and wave it over him?'

'Couldn't you say "Abracadabra" and see if that works?'

'Couldn't you find another wizard and ask him what to do?'

'My friends,' said Mr Majeika, 'it's no use. There's nothing else to try. Last night, while I was here alone, I made use of every possible means I know, and I can do nothing. And as to finding another wizard, that would be very hard indeed. There are so very few still working, and we don't know each other's names. It might take me years to find another one, and even then he might not have the answer.'

Class Three went home rather gloomily that day. They had all begun to feel sorry for Hamish Bigmore. 'He's staying with his friends again,' Thomas and Pete told their mother.

The next day was Friday. Hamish Bigmore's parents were due to come home that evening.

Half-way through morning school, Jody suddenly put up her hand and said: 'Mr Magic?'

'Yes, Jody?'

'Mr Magic, I've got an idea. You said that things *sometimes* happen like they do in fairy stories. I mean, like Cinderella's coach turning back into a pumpkin.'

'Yes, sometimes,' said Mr Majeika, 'but as you've seen with Hamish, not always.'

'Well,' said Jody, 'there is something that I wondered about. You see, in fairy stories people are often turned into frogs. And they always get turned back again in the end, don't they? And I've been trying to remember *how*.'

Jody paused. 'Go on,' said Mr Majeika.

'Well,' said Jody, 'I *did* remember. Frogs turn back into princes when they get kissed by a princess.'

Mr Majeika's eyes lit up. 'Goodness!' he said. 'You're absolutely right! Why didn't I think of that? We must try it at once!'

'Try what, Mr Magic?' asked Pandora Green.

'Why, have Hamish Bigmore kissed by a princess. And then I do believe there's a very good chance he will change back.'

'But please, Mr Magic,' said Thomas, 'how are you going to manage it? I mean, there's not so very many princesses around these days. Not as many as in fairy stories.'

'There's some at Buckingham Palace,' said Pandora.

'But they don't go around kissing frogs,' said Thomas.

'You bet they don't,' said Pete. 'You

see pictures of them in the newspapers doing all sorts of things, opening new hospitals, and naming ships, and that sort of thing. But not kissing frogs.'

'Are you sure, my young friend?' said Mr Majeika gloomily.

'Quite sure,' said Thomas. 'Unless they do it when nobody's looking. I mean, it's not the sort of thing they'd get much fun out of, is it? Frog-kissing, I mean.'

'I bet,' said Pete, 'that a real live princess wouldn't do it if you paid her a thousand pounds.'

'Just imagine,' said Thomas, 'going to Buckingham Palace, and ringing the doorbell, and saying: "Please, have you got any princesses in today, and would they mind kissing a frog for us?" They'd probably fetch the police.'

'Oh dear,' said Mr Majeika. 'I'm afraid you're right.'

Nobody spoke for a long time. Then Mr Majeika said gloomily: 'It seems that Hamish Bigmore will have to remain a frog. I wonder what his parents will say.'

'Please,' said Jody, 'I've got an idea again. It may be silly, but it *might* work. What I think is this. If we can't get a real princess, we might *pretend* to have one. Make a kind of play, I mean. Dress up somebody like a princess. Do you think that's silly?' She looked hopefully at Mr Majeika.

'Not at all,' said Mr Majeika. 'We've nothing to lose by trying it!'

Which was how Class Three came to spend a good deal of the morning trying to make the room look like a royal palace in a fairy story. They found the school caretaker and persuaded him to lend them some old blue curtains that were used for the play at the end of term. And Mrs Honey, who taught the nursery class, agreed to give them a box of dressing-up clothes that the little children used. In this were several crowns and robes and other things that could be made to look royal.

Then there was a dreadful argument about who was to play the princess.

Jody said she ought to, because it had all been her idea. Pandora Green said *she* should, because she looked pretty, and princesses always look pretty. Mr Majeika tried to settle it by saying that Melanie should do it, as she was the only girl in the class who hadn't asked to. But Melanie, who hated the idea of kissing a frog, started to cry. So in the end Mr

Majeika said that Jody should do it after all, and the other girls could be sort-of-princesses too, only Jody would play the chief one.

Then they got ready. A kind of throne had been made out of Mr Majeika's chair, with one of the blue curtains draped over it. Jody wore another of the curtains as a cloak, and one of the crowns, and a lot of coloured beads from the dressing-up box. And all the other girls stood round her.

Mr Majeika turned out the classroom lights and drew the curtains. Then he said he thought they ought to have some music, just to make things seem more like a fairy story. So Thomas got out his recorder, and played 'God Save the Queen' and 'Good King Wenceslas', which were the only tunes he knew.

They didn't seem quite right for the occasion, but Mr Majeika said they would have to do. Then he told Jody to start being the princess, and say the sort of things that princesses might say in fairy stories.

Jody thought for a moment. Then she said in a high voice: 'O my courtiers, I have heard that in this kingdom there is a poor prince who has been enchanted into a frog by some wicked magician.' She turned to Mr Majeika and whispered: 'You're not wicked, really, Mr Magic, but that's what happens in fairy stories, isn't it?'

'Of course,' said Mr Majeika. 'Please continue. You are doing splendidly.'

'O my courtiers,' went on Jody, 'I do request that one of you shall speedily bring me this frog. For I have seen it written that should a princess of the blood royal kiss this poor frog with her own lips, he will regain his proper shape.' She paused. 'Well, go on, somebody,' she hissed. 'Fetch me the frog!'

It was Mr Majeika himself who stepped up to the tank, put in his hands, and drew out Hamish Bigmore. So he did not see the door opening and Mr Potter coming into the room.

'Ah, Mr Majeika,' said Mr Potter, 'I just wanted to ask you if you could look after school dinner again today, because –' He stopped, staring at the extraordinary scene.

Mr Majeika was kneeling on one knee in front of Jody, holding out the frog. 'Go on,' he whispered, 'I feel the magic working.'

'O frog,' said Jody in her high voice,

'O frog, I command you, turn back into a prince!' And she kissed the frog.

'Now, really,' said Mr Potter, 'I'm not at all in favour of nature-study being mixed up with story-times. And school curtains should not be used for this sort of thing. While as to that frog, its proper place is a pond. I'll allow tadpoles in school, but not frogs. They jump out of the tanks and get all over the place. Now, if you'll just hand that one over . . . Where is it?'

'Here I am,' said Hamish Bigmore. He had appeared out of nowhere, and the frog was gone.

Mr Potter sat down very suddenly in the nearest chair. 'I don't feel very well,' he said.

'Ah,' said Hamish Bigmore, 'you should try being a frog for a few days.

Does you no end of good. Makes you feel really healthy, I can tell you. All that swimming about, why, I've never felt better in my life. And being kissed by princesses, too. Not that my princess was a real one.' He turned to Mr Majeika. 'You really should have taken me to Buckingham Palace,' he said. 'I'm sure the Queen herself would have done it, to oblige me.'

Mr Potter got to his feet and left the room, muttering something about needing to go and see a doctor because he was imagining things.

'And now,' said Hamish Bigmore to Class Three, 'I'm going to tell you all about the life and habits of the frog.' Which he did, at great length.

'Oh dear,' said Pete to Thomas. 'He's worse than ever.'

CHAPTER 5

The Disappearing Bottle

It was about three weeks after this that several of Class Three went to see a film about Superman.

'The best bit,' said Jody to Pete and Thomas, 'was when he flew right over those tall buildings. I'd love to be able to fly like that. Do you think people ever can?'

'I shouldn't have thought so,' said Pete. 'But you could ask Mr Magic. I'm sure he'd know.'

So, when Class Three were beginning their next lesson, Jody did ask him: 'Mr Magic, can you really fly, like Superman?'

Mr Majeika smiled at her over his glasses. 'If you mean *me*, then certainly not! I'm too old for such things. But someone a bit younger could manage it, with a little help.'

'Do you mean a little magic?' asked Jody. Mr Majeika nodded.

'Rubbish!' shouted Hamish Bigmore. 'You couldn't make *anyone* fly, Mr Magic. No one could. It's scientifically impossible.' Since the business of the frog, Hamish Bigmore had been behaving worse than ever. Obviously he thought Mr Majeika wouldn't dare to do anything else to him.

Mr Majeika sighed wearily. 'It is not rubbish, Hamish Bigmore, but I don't intend to waste time showing you.'

'Oh do, please *do*,' said Jody, and soon there was a chorus of: 'Yes, *do*, Mr Magic! Couldn't you, just *once*?'

'Of course he can't,' sneered Hamish Bigmore.

'Very well then,' snapped Mr Majeika, 'just to prove Hamish Bigmore wrong, I will. But it will have to wait until tomorrow, when I can bring the potion.'

Everyone fell silent, wondering what 'the potion' was.

When the next day came, Mr Majeika seemed at first to have forgotten all about his promise, for he said nothing about it. At last Jody asked him: 'Did you bring the flying potion, Mr Magic?'

Mr Majeika frowned. 'Well, yes, I did. But really I think the whole idea is a mistake. I'd much rather we forgot all about it. These things have a way of getting out of hand . . .'

'There you are!' jeered Hamish Bigmore. 'I told you he couldn't do it.'

'Oh, really, Hamish Bigmore, you're enough to try the patience of a witch's broomstick,' grumbled Mr Majeika. 'I suppose I'll *have* to do it just to keep you quiet.'

'Do what, Mr Magic?' asked Thomas.

'Why, give you all some of the flying potion,' said Mr Majeika.

There was a happy uproar. 'What, all of us?' asked Pete. 'Are we all going to be able to fly?'

'Well, it'll have to be all or none,' answered Mr Majeika. 'Can you imagine how jealous everyone would be if I only let one or two of you do it? But it won't be proper flying, mind. Just a little hover in the air. The potion is far too precious to be wasted.'

Class Three tried to make him change his mind and allow them to fly properly, but he wouldn't. So in the end they queued up, and were each given a very small spoonful by Mr Majeika. It was green and sticky, and tasted like a rather nice cough mixture. Only Hamish

Bigmore refused to have any; he said the whole idea was silly.

As soon as they had taken it, Class Three began to jump up and down, in the hope of taking off into the air. But nothing happened.

They were all dreadfully disappointed.

'There you are!' sneered Hamish Bigmore. 'I told you so! It doesn't work!'

'Oh, but it does,' said Mr Majeika. 'I forgot to tell you that it takes exactly half an hour before anything happens. So we must get on with the lesson for the next half-hour, and *then* see.'

It was a very long, slow half-hour, and even when it ended nothing happened to Class Three. 'What's gone wrong?' Jody asked Mr Majeika.

'Nothing,' answered Mr Majeika,

smiling. 'You can't just sit there and expect to fly without *doing* anything.'

'Do you mean we should wave our arms about or something?' asked Pete.

Mr Majeika shook his head. 'No, my friend. The secret is to *think* about flying. If the notion of flying comes into your head, then – hey presto!'

'I'm thinking hard about it,' said Jody. 'I'm thinking about floating up in the air from my desk, and – Oh! *Oh!*' Suddenly she found herself doing just that.

In a moment they were all doing it. It was a very peculiar feeling; you simply had to think about leaving the ground, and you did. What's more, once you were in the air, if you thought about (say) spinning round like a top, you found yourself doing it. Pete said: 'I'm going to think about floating across the room to the door –' and there he was, doing just that.

The only thing that disappointed them was that they were never very far from the floor. 'Can't you let us go higher?' they pleaded with Mr Majeika.

He shook his head. 'Too risky,' he said. 'You might bump your heads on the ceiling, or do all kinds of dreadful things. And anyway, I want to save my precious flying potion. It always wears off in half an hour, however much you take, so it would be an awful waste to give you lots of it.'

Alas, it did wear off in half an hour, to everyone's regret, and all too soon they were down on the ground again, quite unable to float, however much they thought about it.

'Well, my friends,' said Mr Majeika,

'I hope you enjoyed that. And,' he turned to Hamish Bigmore, who had been sitting watching everyone else float through the air, 'I hope *you* believe me now.'

'Oh yes, Mr Magic,' answered Hamish Bigmore, with a rather peculiar smile on his face.

'Very good,' said Mr Majeika. 'Well then, let me put the potion away, and we can get on again with our proper lessons, which today –' He stopped suddenly. 'What's happened to the potion?' he said.

The bottle had vanished.

'*Where is the potion?*' said Mr Majeika again, in an anxious voice. 'It was on my desk. Someone has picked it up and hidden it. Will they please return it at once?'

No one said anything. Mr Majeika turned to Hamish Bigmore. 'Hamish,' he said, 'somehow I have a feeling that *you* are behind this.'

Hamish Bigmore shook his head. 'Oh, no, Mr Majeika,' he said sweetly, 'why should *I* do a thing like that?'

Mr Majeika looked at him steadily. 'Turn out your pockets,' he said to Hamish. But the bottle wasn't in Hamish's pockets.

After that, Mr Majeika searched everyone in Class Three, saying as he did so: 'Oh dear, I *knew* I shouldn't have brought the potion to school. One of you has played a wretched trick on me, and it's quite unfair.'

'Perhaps,' suggested Hamish Bigmore, 'the bottle itself can fly, and it's flown away?' He laughed uproariously, but Mr Majeika was not amused.

Nowhere could the bottle be found, and by the end of school for that day Mr Majeika was looking very worried and very cross.

'I'm sure it *is* Hamish,' said Pete to Thomas. 'He had something tucked under his coat when he left the classroom.'

'Well,' said Thomas, 'I'm sure we'll find out who's got it. Whoever they are, they're bound to start flying pretty soon.'

CHAPTER 6

Mr Potter Goes for a Spin

But no one did. Days went by, then several weeks, and nothing peculiar happened in Class Three. After a time Mr Majeika, who at first had continued to look very worried and cross, stopped seeming to be so unhappy about the loss of his potion.

Eventually he seemed to have forgotten all about it.

The weather gradually began to warm up. One morning, about two weeks before the end of term, it was so hot that Mr Majeika opened the windows in Class Three. For some reason Hamish Bigmore seemed very pleased at this, though no one could make out why.

Mr Majeika was in charge of school dinner that day, and he walked up and down between the tables, making sure that everyone was eating tidily and not making a mess. Hamish Bigmore was being unusually nice to him. 'Oh, Mr Magic,' he kept saying, 'isn't it a lovely day? I do hope you're feeling well today?'

'Yes, thank you, Hamish,' said Mr

Majeika, obviously pleased that Hamish was being polite.

'Is there anything I can get you?' Hamish asked, smiling sweetly. 'I'm sure the dinner-ladies would give me a cup of tea for you if I asked them nicely. Shall I go to the kitchen and see?'

Mr Majeika smiled back at Hamish. 'That's very kind of you,' he said. 'Yes, I would love a cup of tea if they can make me one without too much trouble.' And off went Hamish.

A few minutes later he came back, carrying the tea. 'Here you are, Mr Magic,' he said, still smiling sweetly. 'I do hope you like it.'

'Thank you, Hamish,' said Mr Majeika, putting it down on the table to let it cool before drinking it.

At this moment Mr Potter bustled up.

'Ah, Mr Majeika, I wonder if we could do a bit of a change-round this afternoon? I haven't seen much of Class Three this term, so I'd like to take them after lunch, and you can take Class Four, whom I'd normally be teaching. Will that be all right?'

'Certainly,' said Mr Majeika.

'That's fine,' said Mr Potter, and he was just going when he saw the cup of tea. 'Ah,' he said, rather puzzled. 'I see the dinner-ladies have left my tea out here today. I always have a cup of tea after lunch, you know. Wakes me up!' And with that, he downed the tea at one gulp, muttered 'Far too much sugar,' and hurried back to his office.

Hamish Bigmore had gone rather pale. 'What's the matter?' Pete asked him.

Hamish said nothing. But a moment later, after Mr Majeika had gone off to teach Class Four, he whispered to Pete: 'We're for it now! Really for it!'

'What do you mean?' asked Pete.

'That cup of tea!' said Hamish. 'It was meant for Mr Magic.'

'I know that,' said Pete. 'But I don't think he really minded Mr Potter drinking it.'

'It's not that, you ass,' said Hamish. '*There was flying potion in it*.'

'*What?*' shouted Pete.

'Ssh!' said Hamish. 'I meant it for Mr Majeika. I thought I'd get my own back for being turned into a frog, so I hid the flying potion and meant to make him drink it all one day when the window was open, and I hoped he'd fly away out of the window and never come back.

And now Mr Potter's drunk it instead!'

'Was there a lot in the cup?' asked Pete.

'The whole bottle,' said Hamish gloomily. 'I can't imagine what's going to happen.'

Pete thought for a few moments. Then he said: 'If odd things start to happen to Mr Potter, we'll *all* get into trouble, you can be sure of that. And if he finds out that Mr Magic's flying potion is at the back of it, you can be sure Mr Magic will lose his job, and Class Three will be given an ordinary teacher instead. Now, that may be what *you* want, Hamish Bigmore, but the rest of us certainly don't. So I'm going to warn everyone *not to pay any attention if Mr Potter starts to fly*. It's the only hope . . .'

When Mr Potter arrived to teach Class Three fifteen minutes later, everyone had been warned. They sat silently at their desks, knowing that something very odd was probably going to happen, but determined not to laugh or give any other sign that something extraordinary was going on.

In fact, for a very long time nothing happened at all. Mr Potter began to give them an ordinary, boring lesson, and the afternoon dragged by as slowly as usual.

'It takes half an hour to work,' Jody whispered to Thomas. 'The flying potion, I mean.'

'The half-hour was up a long time ago,' whispered Thomas. 'I can't think why nothing's happening.'

'*I* know,' whispered Pete. 'It's because he's not *thinking* about flying. You've got to think about it in order to leave the ground.'

'Well, let's hope he *doesn't* think about it,' whispered Pandora.

Mr Potter glanced up irritably. 'Stop that whispering at the back!' he said. 'Has any of you been listening to me? What have I been talking about, Jody?'

There was an awkward silence as Jody tried to remember what Mr Potter had been saying. 'It was something about how the wind works, wasn't it?' she asked hopefully.

'Certainly not!' spluttered Mr Potter. 'I have been giving you a lesson on the force of gravity. Do you know what gravity is?'

Jody shook her head.

'Oh, really!' said Mr Potter. 'You haven't been listening at all. Gravity is the thing which keeps us all on the ground, and stops us floating up *into the air . . .*'

His voice became a squeak of surprise on these last three words, for as he spoke them, he himself left the floor and began to rise slowly towards the ceiling.

There were a few snufflings among Class Three as they stuffed handkerchieves into their mouths to stop themselves laughing. But otherwise, silence.

Mr Potter had stopped rising, and was suspended in mid-air, about four feet from the floor. 'Er,' he said, 'something peculiar seems to have . . .' He looked at Class Three, and Class Three looked back at him. No one laughed or said anything. Slowly, Mr Potter came down to the ground.

'He must have stopped thinking about

floating,' whispered Jody. 'Let's make him talk about something else. That should keep his mind off it.'

'Mr Potter,' said Thomas loudly, 'we don't really want to hear any more about the force of gravity. Why not tell us about winds instead?'

'Certainly not!' said Mr Potter crossly. 'Kindly attend to the lesson. As I was saying, gravity stops us from floating in the air. Now you may ask how it is that birds manage to fly? Let me tell you. When birds wave their wings –' He started to wave his arms to show them what he meant; and, as he did so, he rose once more in the air. At first he didn't seem to notice, and simply went on talking.

'By moving their wings,' he said, 'birds create a current of air which permits them to fly wherever they want. They can fly to the left' (and so saying, Mr Potter flew across the classroom) 'or to the right' (he flew back to his desk) 'or round and round in circles.'

As he said these last words, Mr Potter slowly circled the room, and then returned to his desk. He looked puzzled. 'Er,' he said, 'I don't know how to put this, boys and girls, but during the last few minutes, while I was talking to you, I had the strange sensation that . . . well, that *I* was flying like a bird. Did you notice anything odd, boys and girls?'

'Oh no,' said Thomas.

'We didn't see a thing,' said Pete.

'You must have imagined it,' said Jody.

'Only,' said Thomas, 'we wish you'd stop thinking about – I mean talking about – flying, and tell us about something else.'

'Listen, boy,' said Mr Potter crossly, 'I am going to finish my lesson on the force of gravity, and I want no more interruptions from you! Now you must understand that, if it were not for the force of gravity, we couldn't simply walk about on two legs. Why, we'd often find ourselves standing on our heads!' And of course, as he said these words, Mr Potter's feet rose a little from the ground and he slowly turned right over in the air, coming to rest standing on his head.

There was silence. 'Are you *sure* nothing peculiar is happening to me, boys and girls?' came Mr Potter's voice from the floor.

'Oh, nothing at all,' said Pandora

Green. 'You're just standing by your desk as usual.'

'Oh,' said Mr Potter. 'Oh well . . . I really ought to go and see a doctor about these funny things I keep imagining . . . Still, I must finish the lesson.' He cleared his throat. 'Not only would we often find ourselves standing on our heads,' he continued, 'but without gravity we could simply float out through any open window, sail up into the sky, and never come back.'

And of course, exactly as these words left Mr Potter's lips, he left the floor and began to float, still upside-down, towards the open window.

'Quick!' shouted Pete. 'Someone shut the window, or he'll never be seen again.'

Everyone made a rush for the

window. But just at that moment the bell rang for the end of afternoon school; and as it did so, Mr Potter came back to earth with a bump and sat up, rubbing his head.

'Good gracious!' he said. 'What a lot of funny things I have been imagining. Boys and girls, back to your places! I never said you could go yet.'

'The half-hour's up!' whispered Jody. 'The flying potion has worn off. Thank goodness for that!'

The door opened, and in came Mr Majeika. He was holding something in his hand. 'I hope they behaved themselves?' he asked Mr Potter, who nodded rather weakly. 'That's good,' said Mr Majeika. 'I found *this* in the kitchen.' He showed Class Three what was in his hand; it was the empty bottle which had contained the flying potion. 'I just wondered if anyone had been . . . ?' he said, looking at them meaningfully.

Class Three shook their heads.

'Nothing's happened at all, Mr Magic,' said Hamish Bigmore firmly. 'It was just an ordinary lesson. But I think Mr Potter would like a cup of tea to calm his nerves. And no sugar in it this time.'

CHAPTER 7

Dental Problems

'Mr Potter wants everyone to clean their teeth very thoroughly tomorrow,' said Mr Majeika to Class Three, one afternoon about a week before the end of term. 'There's a dentist coming to teach you about careful brushing, and how to fight tooth decay, and Mr Potter says he doesn't want everyone's mouths looking and smelling like the insides of old dustbins.'

'Please, Mr Magic, my teeth are *always* clean,' said a voice. It was Melanie.

'Yes, Melanie, I'm sure they are,' said Mr Majeika. 'But not everyone is as careful as you.'

'Melanie's teeth are *clean* all right,' said Hamish Bigmore. 'But look how ugly they are! They stick out all over the place.'

Unfortunately this was quite true. Melanie did have sticking-out teeth. But of course being told this made her cry even louder than usual. 'Boo-hoo! I hate you, Hamish Bigmore, you're *horrid*!' she wailed.

'Don't you call *me* horrid,' answered Hamish. 'Just think how horrid *you* look, with those teeth. In fact you look just like Count Dracula! Melanie's got teeth like a vampire! Ya, horrid old vampire!'

'Be quiet, Hamish Bigmore,' said Mr Majeika. But Hamish, as usual, wouldn't pay any attention. 'Vampire! Vampire!' he shouted. 'Melanie looks like a vampire!'

Mr Majeika suddenly lost his temper. 'I'll show you who's a vampire!' he cried, and pointed a finger at Hamish.

Hamish Bigmore opened his mouth to say something rude – and then stopped, because everyone was suddenly laughing at him. 'Vampire! Vampire!' they were shouting.

'What's got into you, you sillies?' he

asked them. But they would only answer: 'Vampire! Vampire!'

'Here,' said Pandora Green, 'take a look at this.' She kept a pocket-mirror in her desk for putting on lipstick, when Mr Majeika wasn't looking. Now she held it up to Hamish Bigmore.

He stared in the mirror, then turned on Mr Majeika. 'Look what you've done, Mr Magic!' he shouted.

It was perfectly true. Hamish Bigmore had suddenly grown vampire's teeth.

They were very long and pointed, and stuck right out of his mouth. Two were especially long and sharp. It was as nasty a sight as anything in the horror films on television.

'Oh dear, oh dear,' Mr Majeika was saying. 'I seem to have done it again. These old spells just come back into my head when I least expect them, and then I say them to myself without thinking, and then hey presto! the damage is done.'

'But surely you know how to take *this* spell off him?' asked Jody. 'It can't be as difficult as the frog.'

Mr Majeika shook his head. 'It's quite an easy one,' he said. 'In fact you don't need a spell to get rid of the vampire teeth, I remember that. Hamish himself has to *do* something to have his teeth become normal again. But I can't for the life of me think what it is.'

Hamish Bigmore himself had been sitting silently through this. Now he snarled between his vampire teeth: 'Well, if you can't take these teeth away, I'm going to *use* them. I'll be a real vampire and bite you all! And you know what happens when you're bitten by a vampire? You become a vampire yourself! Ha! ha!'

'Don't be silly,' said Mr Majeika. 'You're not a real vampire. You just happen to have grown a set of vampire's teeth. But I can tell you that if you start behaving in a foolish fashion, Hamish Bigmore, you can be sure of one thing – those teeth will never go away. Just you put a scarf around your face to hide them, and go home quietly, and tell everyone there that you've got toothache, and go straight to bed, and with luck in the morning they'll have gone.'

For once, Hamish Bigmore did as he was told.

But the next morning the vampire teeth were still there. Thomas and Pete could see them the moment Hamish

Bigmore came into Class Three and unwrapped the scarf from around his face. 'Whatever did your mum and dad say?' asked Pete.

'They're away,' said Hamish. 'There's an old aunt of mine looking after me, and she's too short-sighted to notice. Mr Magic should go to prison for doing this to me!'

'It was all your own fault,' said Thomas. 'But what is the dentist going to say?'

This was exactly the thought that crossed Mr Majeika's mind when he arrived in the classroom and saw that Hamish's teeth hadn't changed back in the night. 'Oh dear,' he said, 'this is going to be very awkward.'

When the dentist came, it proved to be a lady. Hamish Bigmore had been put in a far corner of the room, in the hope that she would not look at him, but she went carefully round everyone in the class, making them all open their mouths.

'Now,' she said brightly, peering into Thomas's, 'have you been brushing away regularly with Betty Brush and Tommy Toothpaste? You must remember to fight Dan Decay, and Percy Plaque, or horrid old Terry Toothache will come along and make your life a misery.'

'She's treating us as if we were toddlers in the nursery class,' grumbled Jody. But there was nothing anyone could do to stop the lady dentist chattering away in this daft fashion. Finally she got to Hamish Bigmore, who, on Mr Majeika's instructions, had the scarf wrapped tightly around his mouth.

'Who have we here?' she said brightly. Hamish got to his feet and started to make for the door.

'He's not feeling very well,' said Mr Majeika. 'I think he needs to go to the lavatory.'

'Well, he can just wait a minute,' said the lady dentist firmly. 'Let's unwrap that scarf, my little friend, and see what we find beneath. Are Dan Decay and Percy Plaque lurking there, or have you been a good boy and used Betty Brush and Tommy Toothpaste?'

Hamish Bigmore had had enough of this. He pulled the scarf from his face and bared his horrid long pointed teeth at the lady dentist.

'No,' he cried. 'I haven't been a good

boy! I'm Victor the Vampire and I'm going to drink your blood!'

The lady dentist gave a shrill scream, and rushed from the classroom.

★

'Now really,' said Mr Majeika to Hamish Bigmore when order had been restored, 'that was *not* necessary. You might have given her a heart attack.' As it was, the lady dentist had driven away very fast in her little car, saying she never wanted to look at schoolchildren's teeth again.

'I'm sorry you've still got those teeth,' continued Mr Majeika to Hamish, 'but really, behaving so naughtily won't help. I'm still trying to find out what it is you must do to get rid of them – I've been looking through all my old spell-books – and in the meantime I advise you to be as good as possible . . .' Suddenly he stopped.

'What's the matter?' asked Jody.

'I've just remembered!' cried Mr Majeika in delight. 'I've remembered what Hamish has to do to get rid of those teeth! *He has to be good!*'

CHAPTER 8

Hamish the Good

At first no one could believe it was as simple as that. But in the end Mr Majeika convinced them all. 'I've remembered what I was taught as an apprentice wizard,' he said. 'If anyone gets a horrid affliction or disease as a result of behaving nastily to someone,' he said, 'they have to be *good* for a certain period of time, and it will go away. So Hamish will have to be good until – well, I should think until the end of term should just about do it. What do you think about that, Hamish?'

Hamish Bigmore looked at Mr Majeika gloomily. 'Isn't there an easier way?' he said.

Mr Majeika shook his head. 'I'm afraid not,' he said. 'For the next week or so, Hamish, you will have to behave like an entirely different person. You must become utterly and completely *good*.'

Hamish sat in silence, stunned by this news.

'He'll never manage it,' said Pete to Thomas. 'Not a hope.'

*

But the surprising thing was that, by next day, Hamish obviously *was* managing it.

Up to now, he had always arrived late at school in the morning, with some silly excuse he'd dreamt up. But today Class Three found him already sitting at his desk when they arrived. And when Mr Majeika came into the classroom, he saw that there was a bunch of wild flowers in a jam jar on his table. 'Oh,' he said. 'Did one of the girls put this here?'

There was a general shaking of heads, and Hamish spoke up: 'No, sir,' (he had never called Mr Majeika or any of the other teachers 'sir' before) 'it was me, sir. I picked them from the hedgerow on my way to school. Don't you think they're pretty, sir?'

Mr Majeika looked at Hamish Bigmore suspiciously. 'Don't overdo it,

Hamish,' he said warningly. 'Just being *normally* good, like everyone else, will be quite enough.' But Hamish said nothing.

They began lessons. Normally Hamish Bigmore interrupted Mr Majeika at least once every five minutes, with some silly question or rude comment. But today he was completely silent. Mr Majeika obviously couldn't believe it, for he kept casting uneasy glances in Hamish's direction to make sure he wasn't up to something nasty. But not at all. Hamish was very hard at work, and at the end of the lesson he handed a neatly written workbook to Mr Majeika. Class Three had been asked to write something describing a scene in the country, and Hamish's piece was all about sweet little buttercups, and little woolly lambs jumping about in the meadows. 'Are you trying to pull my leg, Hamish Bigmore?' said Mr Majeika. But once again Hamish made no reply.

It was the same at dinner time. Mr Majeika had explained to Mr Potter and the rest of the school that something peculiar had happened to Hamish's teeth, but they would soon be all right again provided nobody took any notice; so Hamish was allowed to have school dinner with everyone else. Usually he fooled around like mad at dinner time, and made a dreadful nuisance of himself to the dinner-ladies. But today everything was different. He not only ate his own dinner as quietly as a mouse, but after it was finished he began to collect up all the other children's dirty plates, knives, forks, and spoons, saying to the dinner-ladies: 'Oh, *do* let me help! Please, is there anything I can do?'

After a bit, one of the dinner-ladies went to Mr Majeika to complain. 'That boy from your class,' she said, 'is giving us all the creeps.'

'Do you mean his teeth?' asked Mr Majeika.

'No, he can't help those, poor dear,' said the dinner-lady. 'I mean his *interference*. He doesn't mean to be a nuisance, the poor creature, but he keeps fussing round us, trying to *help* all the time, and we can't get the washing-up done. What's wrong with him? The other kids never behave like that.'

Mr Majeika sighed. 'I'm afraid he's suffering from an attack of being good,' he said.

Nor was this the end of Hamish Bigmore's 'helping'. At the end of afternoon school he hurried round to the nursery class, and was soon to be seen 'helping' the little children on with their coats, and holding the door open for the mothers who had come to collect them. Unfortunately nobody in the nursery had been told about Hamish Bigmore's vampire teeth, and the air was soon filled with the screams of terrified mothers. 'It's Dracula himself, risen from the grave!' cried one of the more highly strung ladies. Mr Majeika, summoned to the disturbance, told Hamish Bigmore to stop 'helping', and to go home at once, but the damage was done, and it was several days before some of the mothers would venture out of doors again with their toddlers.

Every day for a week, Hamish Bigmore thought of some new way of 'helping' someone at St Barty's, and by the end of the week everyone in the school was a nervous wreck. Everyone, that is, except Mr Potter. Somehow Hamish's good deeds had failed to cause any trouble to the head teacher.

On the last morning of term, Hamish Bigmore arrived at school with his teeth looking perfectly normal again. And there was a gleam in his eye. 'Well, I think I've managed it,' he said to Pete and Thomas.

'Your teeth?' they said. 'Yes, you have. They look quite ordinary again. Mr Majeika was right, then – it worked.'

'No, not *that*, idiots,' said Hamish Bigmore scornfully. And his 'goodness' seemed to have vanished now that his teeth were back to normal. 'Just you wait and see what I mean.'

The day ended with the whole school gathered in the assembly hall to listen to Mr Potter. 'I want you all to enjoy your holidays,' he said. 'But before you go, there's one last thing. Those of you who have been at St Barty's for some time will know that on the last day of the Easter term I always give a prize, the Headmaster's Medal for Good Conduct. And as you may also know, beside the medal there's also ten pounds in cash for the boy or girl who wins it. Each year I look for one boy or girl whose behaviour has been really good, and who has tried to be a real help to everyone at the school. And this term, I have no hesitation in awarding the prize to – Hamish Bigmore.'

There was a gasp of surprise and, especially from Class Three, a howl of rage.

'So *that's* what he was up to,' gasped Pete. 'He didn't care about the teeth at all – he just wanted the money! Well, of all the –'

'Jolly well done, Hamish Bigmore,' said Mr Potter, hanging the medal round Hamish's neck and giving him an envelope containing the money.

'Thank you, *sir*,' said Hamish Bigmore. And he stuck out his tongue at Class Three.

After it was all over, everyone crowded round Mr Majeika. 'Wasn't that wicked of Hamish Bigmore?' Jody asked him. 'Did you know what he was up to?'

Mr Majeika shook his head. 'I'd never

heard of this Good Conduct Medal,' he said, 'or I might have guessed. Why, for two pins I'd turn that medal into a toad!'

'Oh, go on, Mr Magic, please do!' they all said. But he shook his head.

'No, my friends. No more magic, at least not this term.'

'Will you be here *next* term, Mr Magic?' Jody asked excitedly.

Mr Majeika nodded.

'Hooray!' they all said. And then Thomas added as an afterthought:

'Well, don't let Hamish Bigmore ever be *good* again. It's more than we can bear!'

Mr Majeika and the Music Teacher

With thanks to Mrs Bennetts and the school orchestra, and Mrs Jenks and her class, at St Philip and St James School, Oxford, for their help with the story. And in memory of Lucy Tsancheva (1972–1984), who helped so much with the first *Mr Majeika*.

CHAPTER I

Hamish Goes Shopping

Hamish Bigmore's parents sat having breakfast, and looking at a letter.

'Pass the butter!' shouted Hamish, who was just as rude at home as he was at school. 'I said, *pass the butter*!'

'Ooh, sorry, dear,' said Hamish's

mother. She always gave Hamish everything he wanted, and never complained at his rudeness. Of course this made him worse than ever.

'WILL YOU PASS THE BUTTER!!!' Hamish yelled, because his father was still reading the letter, and hadn't handed the butter dish down the table.

'Terribly sorry, old chap,' said Mr Bigmore, giving his son the butter. 'I was busy reading this. Here, have a look.' He handed his son the letter.

Hamish looked at it. This is what it said.

Dear Parents,

I am sure you will be pleased to know that next term I shall be joining the staff of St Barty's School as music teacher. I am going to form a school orchestra, and I want everyone to play an instrument in it. Please make sure that your son or daughter brings an instrument to school with them.

Yours sincerely
Wilhelmina Worlock

Hamish yawned. 'What a boring letter,' he said. 'Pass the toast. I said, PASS THE TOAST!!!' His mother hastily gave it to him.

'Why is it boring, old chap?' asked Mr Bigmore. 'I'd have thought you would want to play an instrument. You always like making a lot of noise.'

'NO I DON'T!' shouted Hamish at the top of his voice. 'And anyway,' he went on, stuffing his mouth full of toast while he spoke, 'plgghhng thrr rrccrrddrr zzz zzhllly.'

'I'm sorry, dear,' said his mother timidly, 'but we can't quite understand what you're saying. Perhaps if you swallowed that toast before speaking . . . ?'

Hamish glared and spat out toast. 'What I said was, playing the recorder is silly. You know, "Twinkle, Twinkle, Little Star", "Baa, Baa, Black Sheep" – that's all just rubbish for babies.' He crammed some more toast into his mouth.

'I suppose so, old chap,' said his father. 'Could you pass me the milk jug, old fellow, if you please?'

'No,' grunted Hamish. 'I'm busy eating.'

Hamish's father got up and fetched the milk jug for himself. 'But you know,' he said, 'they may play grown-up tunes in the orchestra. This Miss

Worlock doesn't say anything about "Twinkle, Twinkle, Little Star". And she doesn't mention recorders. As far as I can see, she'll let you play anything you like.'

Hamish thought for a moment. 'Well, what else *is* there?' he asked.

'I suppose you could play the violin,' said his father.

'Violins are *silly*,' sneered Hamish.

'Or a clarinet,' said his mother.

'That's just a silly sort of recorder with knobs stuck on it,' said Hamish. 'You can't fool me.'

'A flute makes a very pretty noise,' said his father.

'Pretty!' sneered Hamish. 'I don't want to play anything pretty.'

'No, I'm sure not, dear,' said his mother hastily. 'But don't worry. I'm sure we can find something for you. After all, think of all the instruments there are in orchestras – trumpets, oboes, cellos, horns, harps, double basses –'

'Double basses?' said Hamish. 'What are they?'

'Oh, very big things,' said his father. 'Far too big for someone your age. They're very tall, like huge violins, and they make a deep noise when you pluck them or play them with a bow. But if I were you I'd choose a –'

'I WANT A DOUBLE BASS!!!' shouted Hamish Bigmore.

★

'Music teacher?' said Mr Potter, the headmaster of St Barty's Primary School. 'What music teacher? I don't know anything about any music teacher.'

It was the first day of term, and Mr

Potter's office had filled up with angry parents.

'I just can't afford to get expensive musical instruments for my children,' grumbled the mother of Melanie, one of the children in Class Three. 'It costs too much. Who does she think she is, this new music teacher?'

'Yes,' said the other mums and dads crossly, 'you never told us about her.'

'And no one told *me*,' said Mr Potter. '*I* don't know anything about a new music teacher. Here, let me see the letter.'

Someone passed him the letter from Miss Wilhelmina Worlock. 'What a very curious name,' said Mr Potter, looking at it. 'I didn't ask her to come to St Barty's. I wonder who did?'

★

There was a dreadful amount of noise going on in Class Three. Squeaks, grunts, groans, rattles, thumps and whistles. Everyone was playing their musical instruments.

'Do be quiet,' called out Thomas to everyone else. 'I can see Mr Majeika coming down the passage.'

'If he hears all this racket,' said Pete, who was Thomas's twin, 'I'm sure he'll turn us all into frogs or snakes or something. You know what he can do when he's *really* cross.'

Mr Majeika was the Class Three teacher, and he had once been a wizard, though he didn't want anyone to know this. Last term he had lost his temper twice with Hamish Bigmore. The first time he had turned a ruler that Hamish was holding into a snake. The second time he had turned Hamish himself into a frog. Mr Majeika didn't mean to do things like that; he said he'd given up magic, and was trying to be an ordinary teacher. But sometimes he forgot himself, and things happened.

'Good morning, everyone,' said Mr Majeika, coming into the classroom. 'I hope you all had a good holiday. But what was all that noise, and why have you all got musical instruments?'

'It's the new music teacher,' said Jody. 'She wrote to our mums and dads.'

'But Mr Potter doesn't know anything about it,' said Thomas.

'And my mum won't buy an instrument for me,' said Melanie, who was always crying. 'Boo-hoo!' She burst into tears as usual.

'It all sounds a bit peculiar,' said Mr

Majeika. 'But I suppose it will be good for you all to learn some music.'

'I've got a penny whistle,' said Jody, playing a few notes on it.

Other voices spoke up round the class:

'I've got a trumpet my mum bought from a junk shop, but I can't play it yet.'

'I've got a violin, and my dad says he'll teach me.'

'I've got my sister's old guitar.'

'All right,' said Mr Majeika. 'That'll do for now. Put everything away, until this music teacher arrives. And now get your workbooks out and –'

He was interrupted by an odd sort of bumping noise at the door of the class-room. He went over and opened the door.

The doorway was blocked by something very big, made of wood.

'What on earth is this?' said Mr Majeika.

A voice spoke from behind the big wooden thing: 'It's my double bass.' It was Hamish Bigmore.

'Good gracious!' said Mr Majeika. 'Well, you'd better not bring it in here.'

But already Hamish had staggered into the classroom, clutching the enormous musical instrument.

Behind him marched his proud mother and father. 'We always want him to have the best of everything,' said Hamish's father.

'And he *asked* for a double bass,' said Hamish's mother. 'So of course we *had* to get him one.'

Hamish dropped the double bass carelessly on to the floor, and then fell over it.

'Careful, old man,' said his father. 'It cost a lot of money, you know.'

'Shut up, silly!' said Hamish Bigmore. 'It's *my* double bass, and I can do what I like with it.'

'Hamish Bigmore,' said Mr Majeika, 'don't speak to your parents in that fashion. Leave that thing where it is, and sit down in your place. Mr and Mrs Bigmore, I would be obliged if you could remove this musical instrument from the classroom. I can't imagine that the music teacher, whoever she is, will want to have such an object in her orchestra. Apart from anything else, your son isn't big enough to play it.'

'Rubbish!' shouted Hamish Bigmore. 'Of course I am. And of course Miss Worlock will want me to play it. You see if she doesn't.'

Thomas and Pete felt certain that Mr Majeika would lose his temper. In fact he had turned quite white. But he didn't seem angry at all. Instead, he seemed to be frightened.

'Miss – what did you say?' he asked Hamish in an odd sort of voice.

'Miss Worlock,' said Hamish. 'The new music teacher. Miss Wilhelmina Worlock.'

'Wilhelmina Worlock?' said Mr Majeika, putting his hand on his head as if he had a headache. 'Oh, *no*!'

'What's the matter?' asked Pete. 'Have you heard of her?'

'Heard of her?' answered Mr Majeika.

'Oh yes, I've heard of her. I've heard of her all right. Wilhelmina Worlock is a witch.'

CHAPTER 2

The Letter on the Mat

It was Jody who found the letter. She was passing the main door of the school at break time, and she saw it lying on the mat, as if it had just come through the letter-box. It was addressed in spidery handwriting:

To Mr Potter
Head Teacher
St Barty's School
URGENT
Anyone who delays this letter from arriving
FAST will be turned into a TOAD.

Jody thought this last bit was very odd, but she supposed she had better take it to Mr Potter's office at once.

She knocked on the door. 'What is it?' grumbled Mr Potter. He had forgotten all about the mysterious matter of the music teacher, and was trying to add up the term's dinner and swimming money, and wondering why it came out differently every time.

'A letter for you, Mr Potter,' said Jody, handing him the envelope. 'It looks a bit funny to me.'

'Funny?' said Mr Potter crossly. 'What's funny about a letter? I don't see anything funny at all.' He ripped the envelope open crossly.

What happened next was very strange indeed. Something that looked like a photograph fell out of the envelope on to Mr Potter's desk. It was a picture of an old woman with long, straggly, grey hair and gold-rimmed glasses. Jody thought how ugly she looked. Then suddenly the picture began to grow – not just to get bigger, but to become fatter, so that it was no longer a picture at all but a real person. In a moment, the old woman herself was standing in Mr Potter's office.

'Good gracious,' said Mr Potter, scratching his head. 'Where did you come from, madam?'

'In the post, dearie,' said the old lady cheerfully. 'A nice cheap way to travel, for those of us who can manage it. You get a comfy night's rest in an envelope, and then, hey presto, there you are at your destination! And it only costs a first-class stamp. *Much* less fuss than a broomstick. But I forgot – my card.'

She held her hand up in the air, and in it, from nowhere, there suddenly appeared a small white card. She handed it to Mr Potter. 'There you are, dearie,' she said.

Mr Potter looked at it. It read:

WILHELMINA W. WORLOCK
DipW, LRCW
Music Teaching For All Ages
on the So-Spooky Method
Terms: Cash Weekly

Mr Potter scratched his head. 'Would you be the lady who sent out letters to the parents?' he asked.

'That's right, dearie,' said Miss Worlock.

'Ah,' said Mr Potter thoughtfully. He turned to Jody. 'I need to have a word with Miss – Miss Worlock in private,' he said.

'Yes, Mr Potter,' answered Jody, and ran off to tell Class Three the extraordinary thing she had seen.

'Now,' said Mr Potter, closing the door of his office, 'I'm afraid there is some misunderstanding, my good lady. I didn't arrange for you to come and teach music, and I shan't be able to take you on to the staff. I'm sorry you've been troubled. Good day to you.'

He held out his hand. But Miss Worlock didn't shake it. She just giggled: 'Tee-hee!'

'Ugh!' cried Mr Potter, springing back. In his hand was a live toad.

He put it hastily on to his desk and wiped his hand on his trousers. Miss Worlock picked it up and stroked it. 'Come to Mother,' she said cooingly. 'Didn't nasty man like you?'

'As I was saying,' said Mr Potter, breathing heavily, 'we don't require you here. Would you please take yourself off the school premises?' He opened the office door to show her out.

'Tee-hee!' said Miss Worlock.

'Ow!' said Mr Potter, because his hand had begun to sting. He tried to take it off the door-handle. It wouldn't come. It was stuck fast.

'Did you say you wanted me to go? And that you didn't want me to teach music, eh?' said Miss Worlock, pushing her beady eyes unpleasantly near Mr Potter's face. He tried to back away but couldn't, being still stuck to the door.

'That's right,' said Mr Potter uncomfortably. 'We have no need of you here. So kindly be on your way right now.' With his free hand, he pointed at the open doorway – and then cried out, 'Ugh!' again. On the end of his finger was a large black spider.

'Take it off!' yelled Mr Potter, who, even though he was a headmaster, was terrified of spiders.

'Tee-hee!' said Miss Worlock. 'It can stay there, and you can stay stuck there, till you decide that Wilhelmina Worlock is just the person you need to teach music at St Barty's School.'

*

'And she came out of the envelope,' said Jody breathlessly, 'and grew and *grew*, and there she was just standing there, and she looks horrid, just like a witch!'

Mr Majeika nodded gloomily. 'That sounds exactly like Wilhelmina Wor-lock,' he said.

'Do you know her well?' asked Thomas.

'All too well,' said Mr Majeika miserably. 'A particularly nasty type of witch. In fact a horrid old crone, not to put too fine a point on it.'

'But you were a wizard,' said Thomas, 'and *you* didn't do horrid things, did you?'

Mr Majeika shook his head. 'I was a

white magician,' he explained. 'Wilhelmina Worlock does black magic – or at least fairly dirty grey. I wouldn't want to set eyes on her again.' He shuddered.

'Well,' said Pete, 'I expect Mr Potter will soon get rid of her.'

'I wonder,' said Mr Majeika.

*

Mr Potter was still trapped in his office with Miss Worlock. He had agreed that she could teach music at St Barty's, in return for which she set him free from the door-handle and took the spider off his finger. 'Pretty little thing,' she cooed at it, tucking it into her pocket. 'Now,' she said briskly to Mr Potter, 'I want you to pay me a hundred pounds a week.'

'Ridiculous!' spluttered Mr Potter. 'Thirty pounds for two mornings' work is all I can possibly manage.' He took out his handkerchief to mop his head – and found to his horror that it was full of big slimy worms.

'Uggh!' he cried, shaking them on to the carpet.

Miss Worlock gathered them lovingly, and put them in her pocket along with the toad and the spider. 'Aren't they sweet?' she purred.

'Well, fifty pounds,' said Mr Potter, and sat down wearily in his chair – leaping to his feet almost at once, because a live crab, appearing from nowhere, had attached its claws to his bottom. 'Ow!' he cried. 'I've had enough of this! Take a hundred pounds a week, then, you wretched woman, though goodness knows how I can pay you. But get out of my office!'

'Tee-hee!' said Miss Worlock. 'Don't

worry, dearie, I'm off! But you never asked about the letters on my card.'

'Letters?' said Mr Potter weakly.

'DipW,' said Miss Worlock, 'and LRCW. My qualifications. They stand for "Diploma in Witchcraft" and "Licensed by the Royal College of Witches". But I expect you could have guessed that by now. Tee-hee! Bye-bye!'

CHAPTER 3

The Orchestra

'What I don't understand,' said Jody gloomily, 'is why a witch should want to come to St Barty's.'

'Mr Majeika thinks it's probably for the same reason that *he* came,' said Thomas. 'He says you can't make any money as a magician these days. You've got to get some other job. But it's an awful pity that she chose St Barty's.'

They were walking across the playground to the school hall for the first rehearsal of Miss Worlock's orchestra.

'Here,' shouted a voice, 'give me a hand with my double bass.' It was Hamish Bigmore.

Thomas and Pete, who only had recorders to carry, unwillingly picked up the big instrument. 'Quick march!' snapped Hamish. 'Get on with it.'

'*You're* only carrying the little end,' grumbled Pete.

In the hall, Miss Worlock was putting music on the music-stands. 'Ugh,' muttered Thomas, 'I think she looks *horrid*.'

'Not at all,' said Hamish. 'I think she

looks very nice indeed. Not like silly old Mr Majeika.'

One by one, the other children arrived. 'Quiet, everyone!' called Miss Worlock when they were all there. 'I am your new music teacher.' She smiled a horrible smile. 'You may like to know a little about my method. There are all kinds of ways of teaching music. There's the Sol-Fa method. That means you learn the names of the notes: Doh, Ray, Me, Fa, Sol. That's all rubbish, and I don't want to waste time with it. There's also the Suzuki method. That was invented by a Japanese person, and we're not in Japan, so we don't want to know about that. *My* method is called the So-Spooky method. Can anyone guess what *that* means?'

There was silence. Only Class Three

knew that Miss Worlock was a witch, but everyone could see she was a thoroughly nasty person.

'The So-Spooky method,' went on Miss Worlock, 'means that you've got to practise your instruments very hard, otherwise something oh-so-spooky will happen to you. Have you got that clear? Very well, let's get on with the music.'

Everyone picked up their instruments.

'This term,' said Miss Worlock, 'we're going to learn a piece of music called *The Carnival of the Animals*. We'll begin straight away. And I want you to play the right notes, or else . . .'

She sat down at the piano. 'The first piece is a March,' she called out. 'Off we go. One, two, three, four.'

She began to play.

A terrible noise rose up all round the hall. Recorders squeaked like mice caught in a trap, violins scraped like rusty door-hinges, clarinets howled like dogs calling to the moon, trumpets blared like lorries hooting in a traffic jam. 'STOP!' shouted Miss Worlock after a moment. 'That's *terrible*! Didn't you listen to my warning? Now, play the right notes, or you'll know what the So-Spooky method means soon enough. Off we go again. One, two, three, four.'

This time the noise was even worse. 'Eee-ooo-uuu-iii-eee!' squeaked the recorders. 'Zzee-zzii-zzyy!' scraped the violins. 'Wwoo-wwuu-wwoo!' howled the clarinets. 'Raa-raa-raaaaaaaa!' blared the trumpets.

'That's ENOUGH!' screamed Miss Worlock. 'Toads! That's what I ought to turn you into! Horrid slimy toads, every one of you! I've never heard such a noise in all my life.'

A hand went up at the back. It was Jody. 'Please, miss,' she said, 'it's not *our* fault. You told us to get instruments, and bring them to school, but you haven't taught us how to play them properly. Most of us have never done music before.'

'That's right,' murmured everyone. 'We just don't know how to play.'

Miss Worlock glared at them. 'Well then, teach yourselves!' she snarled. 'You're not babies. Take the instruments home, and *find out* how to play them. If you can't discover by yourselves, then get a *book*. You idiots! Any questions?'

'Yes, miss.' It was a rather cheeky girl from Mr Majeika's class called Clare.

'You're the music teacher, so you're supposed to teach us, aren't you?'

'Do you want to be turned into something very nasty?' sneered Miss Worlock at her. 'No? Then don't be rude. Any more complaints?'

'No complaints at all,' said a voice from the back of the orchestra. It was Hamish Bigmore. 'Anyone can play properly if they try. Look!' And he began to saw away at his double bass, *pom pom, pom pom, pom pom, pom pom.* It was just the same two notes, again and again. He had propped the big instrument up in a corner, and was using two hands on the bow – he wasn't nearly tall enough to reach the top of the strings and change the notes. *Pom pom, pom pom, pom pom, pom pom.*

Everyone began to laugh.

'Silence!' screamed Miss Worlock. 'Well, at least there's one person who takes his music seriously. Well done!' she called out to Hamish Bigmore. 'In fact it looks as if you're going to be my star pupil.'

*

After that, Miss Worlock made the orchestra practise for hours and hours every morning, even though Mr Potter said that music was only supposed to be on Thursdays. But all he got for his trouble was a pocket full of black beetles. Miss Worlock told him she'd think of something nastier if he didn't shut up. He went to his office and locked the door, to hide from the horrible music teacher. He tried to work out how he could find a hundred pounds to give her each week. In the end he decided to sack two of the dinner-ladies, and give her their wages. But that meant that he had to serve out dinner himself.

The worst time for the children in the orchestra wasn't, however, the practices with Miss Worlock, but the weekend. Thomas and Pete took their recorders home with them, because Miss Worlock had told the orchestra that everyone must practise hard on Saturday and Sunday. At first they forgot all about it and went off to play football, or on bike rides. However, by lunch time on Saturday, Pete complained to Thomas that his fingers were itching very nastily.

'Mine too,' said Thomas. 'I wonder if it's chickenpox.'

Then, almost by chance, Thomas picked up his recorder, when he was looking for something in the sitting-room, and the itching stopped. He called Pete, and Pete found that *his* itchy fingers stopped when he picked up *his* recorder.

'Oh dear,' said Pete, 'I'm afraid that this is her So-Spooky method. She's going to *make* us practise.'

Sure enough, on Monday morning everyone else complained that they'd itched all weekend, till they'd done at least two hours' practice on their instruments.

Because everyone was working so hard at their music, the orchestra was quite a bit better on Monday, and most of the instruments sounded less like animals screaming. But it was still a fairly terrible noise and Miss Worlock looked as angry as ever.

'*Carnival of the Animals* indeed!' she

snarled, after they had tried to play the March yet again. 'The best you'll ever sound like is a herd of elephants.' Then suddenly her eyes lit up. 'Elephants!' she cried. '"The Elephant!"' And she turned to Hamish Bigmore. 'You alone,' she told him, 'are making a nice noise on your instrument. And *you* shall be the star performer. You shall play the solo in the best of all the tunes in *The Carnival of the Animals*, the tune that's called "The Elephant". Listen!'

And Miss Worlock sat down at the piano and played a heavy, lumbering tune that certainly sounded very like an elephant walking up and down: '*Rum*-tum-tum, *tum*-tiddle-iddle, *um*-tum-tum-tum . . .'

When she had finished, she turned to

Hamish and said: 'Do you think you can play that?'

Hamish grinned. 'I'm sure I can,' he said, 'if I have some help. Give me two people to change the notes – they'll do' (and he pointed at Thomas and Pete) 'and I'll play "The Elephant" better than you've ever heard it!'

★

And so, much against their will, Thomas and Pete found themselves Hamish Bigmore's slaves. '*We* have to do all the real work,' grumbled Thomas, 'while he just stands there and pulls his bow to and fro.'

They had to stand on chairs, one on each side of the double bass, and, while Hamish sawed to and fro with the bow, they had to do all the tricky work of putting the right strings down with their fingers. Naturally they often made mistakes, and Miss Worlock shouted and screamed at them, and threatened to turn them into toads and other nasty things. Meanwhile she petted Hamish Bigmore, and told him how marvellous he was.

'What I can't understand,' Pete said to Hamish one morning, after they had been sweating for hours at 'The Elephant', 'is why you're being so nice to her. Can't you see she's a horrid old bag who means no good to anyone?'

'Of course I can,' grinned Hamish. 'But just think what *I'm* going to get out of it. She's told me that if I play well in the concert at the end of term, she'll teach me everything.'

'Teach you everything?' repeated Thomas. 'Do you mean music?'

'No, idiot,' sneered Hamish. 'I mean

magic. I'm going to get my revenge on Mr Majeika. By the time I'm finished, I'll have learnt how to turn him into a frog. Just you see!'

CHAPTER 4

Trouble in the Staffroom

'Please,' said Jody to Mr Majeika, 'you must do something. Otherwise Hamish will learn to be a black magician, and we'll none of us be safe.'

'Oh dear!' Mr Majeika said, scratching his head gloomily.

'Surely you want Miss Worlock out of the school as much as everyone else does?' said Pete.

Mr Majeika nodded. 'She's quite impossible,' he said. 'She's taken over the staffroom, and she keeps cooking horrible spells and things in there. None of us dares go in, the smell is so nasty. And we can't get on with teaching our classes, she's always having orchestra practice all the time.'

'Couldn't you get rid of her by magic?' asked Jody. 'I mean, you must know some spells that she doesn't. Wouldn't that get rid of her?'

Mr Majeika looked doubtful. 'Spells are tricky things,' he said. 'They often go wrong, or don't work in the way you intend them to. But I suppose I could have a try . . .'

He set off nervously for the staffroom, Thomas, Pete and Jody following him. He seemed very anxious, and was obviously glad to have them with him.

Outside the staffroom, two of the other teachers were hanging about, looking fed up. 'We want to make some coffee,' one of them said, 'but we can't go in because of *her*.'

Nobody needed to ask who was meant by 'her'. Even in the passage, the smell was terrible. And when Mr Majeika opened the door, clouds of steam and green-looking smoke came billowing out.

'Tee-hee,' said a voice from inside, 'come and have elevenses with Auntie Wilhelmina!'

Anxiously, they all stepped inside. Miss Worlock had taken over the whole room. She had lit a fire in the fireplace, and bubbling on it was a cauldron of foul-smelling stuff, all green and scummy.

'Have a cup of Auntie's Morning Mixture!' said Miss Worlock, who seemed to be much more friendly when she wasn't teaching music. She dipped a mug into the cauldron and handed it to Mr Majeika.

Thomas could see that there were nasty-looking things swimming about in it. 'What is it?' he asked.

'Oh, just a touch of this and a dash of that, dearie. Tee-hee!' said Miss Worlock, pointing at an assortment of half-opened tins scattered around the table. They were labelled, Eye of Newt, Bats' Tongues in Tomato Sauce, Curried Frog Spawn, and Pigs' Ears in

Ditchwater (with added Vitamin C).

'Yuck!' said the children. But Mr Majeika, wanting to be polite, had taken the steaming mug from Miss Worlock.

'One lump or two?' asked Miss Worlock, holding out what looked like a sugar bowl.

'Two, please,' said Mr Majeika – and then he sprang back in horror, as she dropped two evil-looking things into his mug. 'What are those?' he cried.

'Oh, just a little thing I put together myself,' cackled Miss Worlock. 'Black beetles coated with mouldy cheese. I've got a deep freeze full of them at home.'

'I, er, I don't think they would agree with me,' said Mr Majeika unsteadily, putting down his mug. 'Now, er, Wilhelmina, you and I are old acquaintances, I wouldn't exactly say friends, but –'

'Not friends, no, dearie,' Miss Worlock screeched merrily. 'Do you remember the time on Walpurgis Night when I –'

'Don't remind me!' said Mr Majeika, looking pale. 'But what I have come to say is this. St Barty's School already has one wizard, that is, me, and any magic that's to be done here is my concern. There isn't room for two of us. You've no right to come barging in here like this and making such a terrible nuisance of yourself. Now, be a good witch – er, music teacher – and pack your bags and leave us in peace.'

'What a pretty speech!' cackled Miss Worlock. 'And what do you intend to do about it, pray, my fine wizard?'

'Do about it?' asked Mr Majeika anxiously.

'How do you intend to get me out of here, you *white wizard*?' Miss Worlock said these last words so that they sounded the rudest thing in the world.

'Well, that is, er,' muttered Mr Majeika, 'I do have my magic powers.'

'Magic powers? Magic powers?' cackled Miss Worlock. 'You think that *you* can get *me* out of here by magic? Just you try! Tee-hee!' And, with these words, she suddenly flew up into the air and landed on top of the bookcase. 'Go on!' she sneered. 'Show me!'

'Oh dear,' sighed Mr Majeika. 'I was afraid it would come to this. Er, let me think, now. Well, I suppose . . .' And, after considering the matter for a moment, he suddenly flung one hand out in front of him.

From his fingers there leapt a blue flame. It crackled and danced about the room, lighting up Miss Worlock's cooking pot and tins, fizzing round the table and the bookshelves, and finally settling on Miss Worlock herself, who seemed about to go up in flames as the blue fire crackled and sizzled over her from top to toe.

But Miss Worlock merely looked bored, and yawned, and after a few moments the blue fire died away. Mr Majeika seemed tired after the effort of making it, but Miss Worlock was quite unharmed.

'Phosphorescent fire?' she laughed horribly. 'Is that all you can do? Lawks, dearie, you can buy that stuff at Tesco's now. I can see I've got a thing or two to teach you.' And she pointed her finger at Mr Majeika, in just the same way that he had jabbed his arm towards her.

Thomas, Pete and Jody expected poor Mr Majeika to burst into flames. But in fact nothing at all happened and he looked as relieved as they did, and put his hand into his pocket to get a handkerchief to wipe his forehead. Then suddenly he cried: 'Ugh! What's *this*?' And the children could see that his hand was covered with a nasty mess.

'Hamish Bigmore's lunch,' cackled Miss Worlock from the top of th bookcase. 'Or at least, what he left on his plate. Half-chewed sausage, mushy peas, and mashed potato. You'll find it all in your pocket, dearie – by magic!'

It was true. Mr Majeika's pocket had suddenly become full of messy food. 'What a horrid trick,' said Jody. 'But can't you think of something else to do to her, Mr Majeika?'

Mr Majeika sighed, then said: 'Well, this might work.' And he began to chant some strange words in a low voice.

Instantly the room became dark, and a cold wind seemed to blow through it. The children thought they could no longer be indoors. They seemed to have been transported to a cold, bleak moorland, with a storm blowing all around them. Then, in the distance, they heard a terrible howling which all too quickly was getting dreadfully near. In a moment, out of the mist there loomed red eyes. Huge shapes could be seen, and

Jody cried out: 'Wolves!' The dreadful animals howled and snarled as they bounded past the children, and Thomas and Pete expected to see them snatch up Miss Worlock in their jaws and tear her to bits.

But suddenly the mist cleared, and the children saw that they were all still in the staffroom at St Barty's. Miss Worlock, quite unharmed, was sitting on the bookcase, eating from a packet labelled Best Dog Biscuits, Made from Fresh Dog.

'Feeble stuff,' she laughed at Mr Majeika. 'Wolves in the mist! Why, I've seen that sort of thing done better on *Blue Peter*. Having a bit of trouble with your trousers, dearie?'

Mr Majeika looked down anxiously at his trousers. Sure enough, a nasty mess was dripping out of his other pocket. 'Hamish Bigmore's pudding,' said Miss Worlock cheerfully. 'Stewed rhubarb. Any more tricks to amuse me?'

'Oh dear,' sighed Mr Majeika. 'Well, I suppose . . .' And again, he muttered something strange under his breath, and once more the room became dark.

This time they were still indoors, but there was the thump of heavy feet, *thump*, *thump*, *thump*, and a voice chanting familiar words:

'Fee, fi, fo, fum,
I smell the blood of an Englishwoman.
Be she alive or be she dead –'

'Oh, come off it, dearie,' cackled Miss Worlock, and the voice faded and the room became light again. 'Don't give me that old one. Any party conjuror can do *that*. You ventriloquists really have had your day, you know. Why, you should see some of those new computer games. They really can teach us oldies a thing or two! Now, be off with you and don't come interfering with me any more. I'm here to stay, dearie, and you'd better get used to it, tee-hee! By the way, don't you think you ought to change your socks?'

Mr Majeika peered down at his feet. 'Oh dear,' he said. 'There does seem to be something squelchy in them. Not Hamish Bigmore again?'

'That's right, dearie,' answered Miss Worlock. 'The custard from his rhubarb. You'll find it all in your shoes.'

'Ugh!' cried Mr Majeika. 'I've had enough.' And he fled from the staffroom, closely followed by Thomas, Pete and Jody.

'Oh dear,' said Jody, 'there's no stopping her.'

CHAPTER 5

The Concert

Miss Worlock's orchestra practised every day. After Mr Majeika had lost his battle with her, nobody else tried to interfere. Mr Potter kept well away, hidden in his office, except when he came out to serve school dinner. No one else dared to tangle with her, and she was allowed to get on with the music whenever she wanted.

She never exactly became good tempered, but at least she stopped threatening to turn the children into toads if they didn't play well enough. And in fact by now the orchestra was sounding pretty good. Everyone only had to go '*um*-pum-pum, *um*-pum-pum' on their instruments while Hamish Bigmore played the tune of 'The Elephant' on his double bass (with Thomas and Pete doing all the hard work at the top end). But at first the '*um*-pum-pum' had sounded pretty terrible, and now it was pretty good. As a result Miss Worlock was in a good mood most of the time, and anyone who had listened in to the orchestra practice would probably have thought that she was a perfectly ordinary music teacher.

Towards the end of term she put up a notice, which said:

CONCERT

by the ST BARTY'S SCHOOL ORCHESTRA

conducted by

WILHELMINA WORLOCK

Demonstration of the So-Spooky Method

Miss Worlock's star pupil

HAMISH BIGMORE

will play 'The Elephant' on his double bass

All Parents Welcome

Thomas and Pete looked very gloomy as the concert approached. 'I know she'll turn us into toads if we don't work the strings right on Hamish's stupid double bass,' groaned Thomas.

'That's right,' said Pete. 'The whole

thing depends on us. If we do our job properly, he'll play the right notes. But she won't thank us. It's her "star pupil" who'll get the praise. And we know what *that* means.'

'Yes, we know what that means,' said Hamish Bigmore, coming up behind them. 'It means she's going to teach me all her secrets! So if she doesn't turn you into toads during the concert, *I* will afterwards!'

On the evening of the concert, Jody found Mr Majeika walking up and down miserably outside the school hall. 'Isn't there anything you can do?' she asked him sadly.

Mr Majeika shook his head. 'Really, I've tried to think of every trick in the book, but there's nothing that can stop her. It isn't that she's a cleverer wizard than me. It's just that she's got such a nasty mind. She thinks of horrid things I'd never dream of. What can you do against someone like that?'

'Oh, but Mr Majeika,' said Jody, 'do try, *please*!'

★

The hall was full of parents waiting for the concert to begin. They'd all been surprised at how hard their children had practised and they wanted to hear the results.

The orchestra took their seats and sat as quiet as mice. Then in came Miss Worlock, leading Hamish Bigmore. He was dressed in a smart suit and a bow tie, just like someone playing in a real orchestra. He was followed by his double bass. Or rather, he was followed by Thomas and Pete, carrying the double bass for him.

Miss Worlock smiled her horrible smile at the audience who clapped politely. 'Good evening, ladies and gentlemen,' she said. 'Welcome to the first concert by the St Barty's School orchestra, who will demonstrate the success of my So-Spooky method of music teaching. May I introduce my star pupil, Hamish Bigmore, who will play "The Elephant" from *The Carnival of the Animals*? Hamish has been my star pupil this term, and after the concert I shall reward him by teaching him *a lot more*! Tee-hee!' She turned to the orchestra. 'And if you don't all play the right notes,' she snarled at them, 'you know what will happen to you. Toads, every one of you! And as for you two,' she turned to Thomas and Pete, 'worse than toads for you, if you don't play the right notes. I'll make you into insects. So watch it!'

She sat down at the piano, rapped her knuckles on the lid to call for complete silence, then played the first notes of 'The Elephant'. The whole orchestra joined in with her.

'*Um*-pum-pum, *um*-pum-pum,' went the recorders, the violins, the clarinets and the trumpets. And then the double bass began to play: '*Rum*-tum-tum, *tum*-tiddle-iddle, *rum*-tum-tum . . .'

Hamish Bigmore sawed away with his bow. And, up at the top end, Thomas and Pete pressed their fingers on the strings so that he played the right notes.

Everything seemed to be going all too well.

Then Pete, out of the corner of his

eye, noticed the door at the back of the hall opening, and Mr Majeika slipping quietly in. A moment later, Mr Majeika had *vanished* – he didn't go out of the door again, but just disappeared, in an instant!

A few moments later, the trouble started.

Hamish Bigmore, sawing away with his double-bass bow, stopped playing for a moment, then went on again. Miss Worlock glared at him.

'There was a fly on the end of his nose,' whispered Thomas.

'*Rum*-rum-tum, *tum*-tiddle-iddle . . .' And again, Hamish stopped for a moment. This time he slapped the end of his nose. The fly flew off.

Miss Worlock glared at him again. He hastily began to play once more.

'*Rum*-tum-tum –' And a third time he stopped playing, now scratching his nose in fury.

The whole orchestra stopped. Miss Worlock was in a towering rage. 'What's going on?' she screeched at Hamish. 'Why aren't you playing properly?'

'There's – there's a fly on my nose!' stammered Hamish.

'A fly?' Miss Worlock shouted. 'Why should a fly stop you? Get on with it, boy, and if I have any more trouble you know what'll happen to you.'

'But – but I'm your star pupil,' spluttered Hamish. 'You can't do anything nasty to me.'

'Oh, *can't* I?' sneered Miss Worlock. 'That's what *you* think. Let me tell you,

Hamish Bigmore, I'm not going to teach you any of my secrets after this, and if you don't want to be turned into a you-know-what, you'd better not make any mistakes again. Now, back to the beginning everyone.'

She began to play the piano once more, and Hamish and the orchestra joined in. '*Rum*-tum-tum, *tum*-tiddle-iddle . . .'

This time, Hamish didn't stop. But Thomas and Pete could see that he was still having trouble with the fly. He was puffing and blowing out of the corner of his mouth, in an attempt to get it off the end of his nose. But it went on sitting there, walking up and down and tickling him as if it knew perfectly well the trouble it was causing.

The fly walking up and down, and

Hamish puffing and panting as he sawed away with the double-bass bow, was all too much for Thomas and Pete. They began to laugh. And as a result, they started to play the wrong notes for Hamish. In a moment the double bass was making a terrible noise.

At this, the whole orchestra stopped playing and everyone began to laugh. Not just the children, but the parents too. The sight of Hamish still struggling with the fly while trying not to take his bow off the double bass was too much for everyone. '*Rum*-tum-tum' went the huge instrument, but now all the notes were wrong and there was Hamish still sawing away and puffing as if he were trying to cut down a tree.

The laughter got louder and louder.

'Do you know what,' said Pete to

Thomas, 'I think the fly *is really Mr Majeika*! I think he turned himself into it to muck up the concert. Good old Mr Majeika!'

And at that instant, the fly vanished and Mr Majeika appeared again, standing in a corner hidden behind the double bass so that Miss Worlock couldn't see him. 'Ssh!' he said to Thomas and Pete, holding his finger to his lips.

Meanwhile the laughter got louder and louder. 'Enough!' shrieked Miss Worlock in a fury. 'Silence! I warned you all! Toads, I said, and I shall do it! I shall turn every one of you into toads.' She turned to the parents. 'And you too, you ungrateful lot, not appreciating Wilhelmina Worlock and her So-Spooky method. Toads, all of you.' And she began to chant words which Thomas,

Pete and Jody knew all too well were a spell.

At this moment, Mr Majeika turned himself into an elephant.

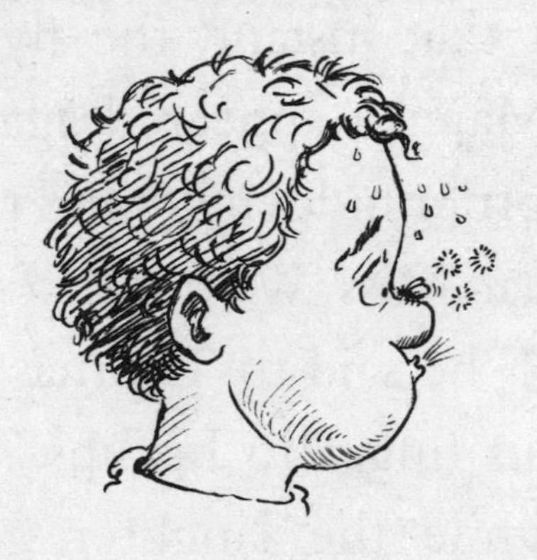

CHAPTER 6

Miss Worlock Catches the Post

'I don't believe it,' gasped Thomas. 'Good old Mr Majeika!'

Jody heard him and guessed what had happened. 'Good old Mr Majeika!' she shouted at the elephant, which waved its trunk at her cheerily.

'It's good old Mr Majeika, come to deal with the wicked witch. Come on, Mr Majeika, you show Miss Worlock who knows the cleverest magic!'

In a moment the whole orchestra was shouting: 'Come on, Mr Majeika!'

The elephant picked its way carefully between the music-stands, and advanced on Miss Worlock.

'No, no!' screamed Hamish Bigmore. Picking up his double bass, he ran at the elephant and banged the huge musical instrument against its side. The elephant turned on him, wound its trunk around the neck of the double bass, and, using it as a cricket bat, dealt Hamish a hefty thump on the bottom. Hamish flew across the hall and landed in the arms of his doting parents, who were sitting in the front row.

'Oh, poor little Hamie!' screeched his mother. 'We must take you out of this rough place at once.' And she and Hamish's father bustled out of the hall, dragging the protesting Hamish, who obviously wanted to stay and see the fun that was starting.

The elephant turned once more on Miss Worlock. But where was she? In an instant, not to be outdone by Mr Majeika, she had turned herself into a rhinoceros with a dangerous-looking horn. It was frightening but also funny because Thomas, Pete and Jody could see that the rhino had Miss Worlock's face – her horrid grin, her straggly long hair, and even her gold-rimmed glasses, which looked ridiculous perched on the end of its nose. 'And the elephant looks just like Mr Majeika,' shouted Thomas. 'It's got his beard and glasses.'

The rhino lowered her horn. 'Oh, watch out, Mr Majeika!' yelled Jody.

But the elephant had already vanished, Mr Majeika obviously thinking that he didn't stand a chance against the wicked-looking rhino with its sharp horn. He had turned himself into, of all things, a motor-bike, presumably so that he could make a fast getaway before he thought of the next move, and in a moment he had roared out of the school hall and into the playground.

Out after him rushed the rhino, with everyone following to see what would happen. There was the motor-bike, revving up in a corner of the playground – and once again, like the elephant, it had Mr Majeika's face, glasses, and beard. But before the children had time to start laughing at this extraordinary sight, the rhino had turned into the most enormous lorry – again, with Miss Worlock's face, hair, and glasses at its front end – and was roaring across the playground to crush the motor-bike beneath its huge wheels.

The motor-bike vanished. 'Oh no!' cried Jody. 'Has she killed him? Poor Mr Majeika, where are you?'

The lorry put on its brakes and screeched to a standstill, obviously uncertain where its enemy had got to. Then suddenly there was a loud hissing, and the lorry sank to the ground quite unable to move.

'What's happened?' shouted Pete. 'Oh, *I* see – clever old Mr Majeika! He's turned himself into a nail, and he's punctured her tyres. She can't move. That's brilliant!'

'Thank you,' said Mr Majeika's voice, as he reappeared in his ordinary shape, standing among the onlookers. 'I think that's going to keep her quiet for a moment. But we've got to think of some way of getting rid of her properly so she just can't come back again. Oh, if only I had time to *think*.' He scratched his head anxiously. 'Oh dear,' he said, 'here she goes again.' And already the lorry had vanished, and Miss Worlock, after reappearing briefly as herself and sticking out her tongue rudely at Mr Majeika, had turned herself into a tiger. 'Not very imaginative,' said Mr Majeika gloomily, 'but it could be nasty.'

'Mr Majeika,' said Jody breathlessly, 'I've had an idea. She came here in an envelope. Do you think we could get her to go away in one?'

Mr Majeika had already turned himself into a lion, but he turned back into himself again for a moment and called excitedly to Jody: 'An envelope? Yes, it's worth trying. Go and get one! And put a stamp on it!' Then he turned into a lion again. Jody rushed off to Mr Potter's office.

The tiger (which of course had Miss Worlock's face) advanced, snarling, on the Majeika-lion, then sprang and sank its teeth into the lion's neck.

The lion vanished, and a groan went up.

'Oh no!' shouted Thomas, 'I think she's got him! This is awful!'

It did indeed seem to be the end of Mr Majeika. There was absolutely no sign of him at all. The tiger sniffed around for a moment, then turned herself back into Miss Worlock.

'Well, my dears,' she said in her nastiest voice, 'I'm afraid poor Mr Majeika has met with a rather nasty accident. We shan't be seeing *him* again. And that should be a warning to everyone not to meddle with Wilhelmina Worlock. I'm afraid our little concert wasn't a great success, but never mind. I'm in charge of St Barty's School now.'

At that moment, Jody came running back into the playground, waving an envelope in her hand. 'I've got it,' she cried. 'And there's a first-class stamp on it.' Then she saw Miss Worlock standing triumphant.

'Be quiet, child!' snapped Miss Worlock. 'As I was saying, I'm in charge here now, and I'm going to rename St Barty's the Wilhelmina Worlock School of Music, on the So-Spooky method, and –' She broke off, crossly. Suddenly she started to scratch herself furiously. 'Dratted flea,' she snapped. 'It must have been on one of the animals. Bother it! It's bitten me. As I was saying – oh, *drat*!' She was scratching like mad now. 'Wretched thing!' she screamed. 'It's biting me all over. Flea bites! I'm covered with them! How can I stop it?'

'Try fly-paper,' called a voice from the far corner of the playground. The children whizzed round to see who was speaking, but there was no one there – though just for a moment they thought they saw Mr Majeika! 'He's alive!' whispered Jody.

'He must be the flea,' whispered Thomas.

Miss Worlock's face had lit up. 'Fly-paper!' she cried. 'What a brilliant idea. Does everyone here know what fly-paper is? That nasty sticky-covered paper that you use for catching flies. Everything sticks to it. It will do the job very well. And if, as I suspect, this flea is really our old friend Mr Majeika – ow! It's biting me again! – then it really will finish him this time. He'll be trapped on it, and I can squash him. Now!' She vanished. And there in her place, waving in the breeze as it flapped around the playground, was a large strip of sticky, yellow fly-paper.

In an instant Mr Majeika had re-appeared. 'Quick! Catch her and roll her up!' he shouted.

Thomas, Pete and Jody rushed on the fly-paper, which of course had the face of Miss Worlock, all flattened. In an instant they had scrumpled and squashed the horrible, sticky paper into a flat bundle.

'But can't she turn herself back again?' panted Pete.

Mr Majeika shook his head. 'Not till she gets untangled,' he said. 'Look, she's in a right old mess! She can't move or recite spells or do anything. It'll take her at least a month, till the stickiness has dried off the paper, for her to wriggle free. Now, quick, into the envelope with her!'

They squashed Miss Worlock into the envelope. 'Now,' said Mr Majeika. He took a pen, and wrote on the front of the envelope:

URGENT

Please send by AIR MAIL

as quickly as possible

to the General Post Office, Timbuctoo

'That should deal with her,' he said cheerily. 'Now, quick, off to the post-box with her – I think I can see the postman coming to empty it now.' Jody took the envelope and ran across the street. She was just in time to catch the post with Miss Worlock. She thought she felt the fly-paper wriggling inside the envelope as she handed it to the postman, but he slipped it into his bag without looking at it and drove off in his van. Jody breathed a sigh of relief.

'Let's hope we don't see the horrid old witch ever again,' said Thomas.

'Look who's coming!' said Mr Majeika.

It was Hamish Bigmore, walking sullenly in through the school gates. 'I've come to fetch my double bass,' he said.

'Star pupil!' mocked Thomas and Pete.

Hamish stuck his tongue out at them. 'Don't you laugh!' he said. 'She didn't teach me everything she knew, but she *did* tell me one very nasty trick and I'm going to do it to you all now. I'm going to fill up your pockets with the most horrid things you can think of, toads and worms and spiders and beetles and crabs and yucky food and everything like that! Now!' And he pointed his finger at them, just like Miss Worlock had done.

They looked down at their pockets.

Nothing happened. But Hamish was

dancing up and down and yelling, and from his own pockets there wriggled all sorts of horrid creatures.

'Something's gone wrong!' he screamed. 'She didn't teach me properly! I've done it to myself! Oh, help!'

And the last they saw of him was a wild figure running off down the road, trying to tear off his coat and trousers as he went.

'Well, well,' said Mr Majeika. 'Perhaps we should be grateful to Wilhelmina Worlock after all. She seems to know how to deal with our Hamish!'

Afterword

As soon as Mr Majeika flies through the window of Class Three's classroom on a magic carpet, we know that a memorable story is about to begin. The story starts well and rushes along with real zest. It is a great mix of the normality of school life and the magic brought to it by a failing wizard forced to earn his living as a teacher. He's the teacher we've all longed for on one of those wet Monday mornings that seem bound to be followed by yet another boring day. Almost without meaning to do it, Mr Majeika is often able to lift the mood of the day and make school a good place to be. There is little time for tears in a school where the teacher is a wizard able to magic up plates of chips. Magic that produces chips really impresses the children – but more impressive is Mr Majeika's acceptance of the blame when the head teacher reminds them that buying chips in the dinner hour is against the rules.

Mr Majeika brings great humour to the stories but he is also rather a serious-minded man, concerned to do the right thing and to keep his job. He has one of the most important qualities for a teacher in that he is always fair. He makes sure, or his almost accidental spells make sure, that the bad are punished. Class Three are naturally thrilled to see the nasty Hamish Bigmore get what he deserves. But even he is dealt with fairly, for Mr Majeika always returns things to normal after the punishing spell has taught him a lesson. When Hamish is given Dracula fangs and can get rid of them only by behaving well, he manages better than anyone could have imagined. So well that he is awarded the Headmaster's Medal for Good Conduct! This reminds us that Mr Majeika doesn't know about all the things that happen in a school, but makes us sure that he'll be back next term, ready to take on Hamish Bigmore once again.

The magic and the laughter run throughout the book, but Mr Majeika is also making a more serious point. He is saying something very important about school and learning: that we learn when our imaginations are touched and when we are having fun. Class Three solve the problem of Hamish the frog by thinking creatively, for this is what Mr Majeika encourages. They remember the magic in traditional stories and work out how to use it in a new situation. Mr Majeika is a good teacher because he sees things from the children's point of view and he knows Class Three will learn if they are interested and if they are given fascinating questions to investigate. When he does use magic, it is never for gain, or for evil. The children respond to his example by offering loyalty and support. Remember how they pretend nothing unusual is happening when the headmaster starts to fly after drinking the flying potion stolen by Hamish. They will not allow Hamish's behaviour to cause trouble for Mr Majeika. Humphrey

Carpenter seems to remember what it was like to be at school and to know how children think; it is this ability to be in touch with children that makes the Mr Majeika adventures such splendid school stories.

★

Humphrey Carpenter has written many books for children and adults. He is an author of enormous talent, famous for his biographies. He has written about C. S. Lewis, the author of the *Narnia* stories that you may have read or seen on TV, and J. R. R. Tolkien, writer of *The Hobbit*, a magical adventure story that you might enjoy reading sometime. Reading children's books was an important part of his research for some of the biographies and Humphrey Carpenter has now become an expert on children's literature. With this background, it is not surprising that he enjoys writing for children. He is proud of the *Mr Majeika* stories and has helped transfer them to the stage and TV. He is also fond of Mr Majeika and has said, in an interview for the *Oxford Times* in 1995, 'He is me and is halfway between the child and the adult world. He sides by instinct with children and is not exactly anti-authoritarian but is quite happy if authority is upset.' With such a central character, the books will always succeed in reminding us that reading really is fun.

The fun continues with the appearance of Mr Majeika's old enemy, Wilhelmina Worlock, in *Mr Majeika and the Music Teacher*, although she introduces quite a serious threat at St Barty's

School. Her magic is not used for good but for self-gain, yet we have a sneaking respect for her clever way of travelling. How brilliant to be able to use the postal service in such a way! The battle between the witch and the wizard brings great excitement to the story and it is very satisfying that Mr Majeika defeats his enemy by turning himself into something as small and seemingly harmless as a flea. His quick-thinking and cleverness outwit Wilhelmina and, this time, even Hamish Bigmore, the witch's star pupil, ends up with just what he deserves.

Good always triumphs in the fast-moving *Mr Majeika* stories. They tell of childhood and of magic and offer reassurance. The wizard teacher, with one foot in the real world and one in a world of magic, intrigues us and has us reaching eagerly for the next of his magical stories.

Wendy Cooling